Metaphorosis

Oct-Dec 2024

Beautifully made speculative fiction

Also from Metaphorosis

Metaphorosis

Oct-Dec 2024

edited by
B. Morris Allen

ISSN: 2573-136X (online)
ISBN: 978-1-64076-284-8 (e-book)
ISBN: 978-1-64076-285-5 (paperback)

Metaphorosis
a magazine of speculative fiction

from
Metaphorosis Publishing

Neskowin

Oct-Dec 2024

A word about E.C. Dorgan

E.C. Dorgan's first story for Metaphorosis ("The Beast Consul") was in our December 2023 issue — the last story in the magazine's eight year run of unsolicited stories (bar one). I ran it there because I thought the story encapsulated all the things the magazine has striven for — beautiful, lyrical prose, engaging characters, and a thoughtful, emotive concept. In this final year, we've published only solicited stories, and I liked Dorgan's writing so much that I asked her back for the magazine's final issue.

I'm happy to say her magic has worked again — though in an entirely different way. Enjoy "The New Western".

The New Western

E.C. Dorgan

I can't think straight with the broncos stampeding up and down the mirrored walls of the elevator, so I press all the buttons and stomp my cowboy boots on the marble. I should be fighting a monster, not stuck in an underground parkade. This city's built on petroleum rivers and decaying dinosaurs, and if I don't find a way out of this elevator, me and my two horses will be bones too. The broncos neigh and I throw my head back with them.

I thought fighting the monster would be easier. In my old life I didn't know he existed. Lightning birthed my broncos and opened my eyes too. I was no one before; I wandered aimless through canola fields without a dream or a destination, only a history I was escaping. I was a trope, a 'woman with a past' in an old western, but on the day of my rebirth, I became something new.

On the day of the change, the sky blackened and the flies surrounding me quieted. I opened my mouth and looked up to the sky. A bolt came down from the heavens and met another one rising up from the earth. They joined in front of me and the world went grey, orange and white. I was deafened and my mouth filled with nitrogen. My legs lost feeling and my stomach emptied.

I rubbed my eyes and found shiny beetles. I looked down and saw two smoking Ready Reckoners. I picked them up and the movement made my arms burn and throb. I rolled up my sleeves and my breath went out of me.

Two flame-coloured horses jumped out of my elbow crooks and raced down my forearms. They started out tiny, but grew bigger with each step. By the time they leapt from my fingers, they were giant beasts. Their hooves sparked on the dry earth and my heart thumped in time with their galloping. The earth heaved under their weight. For the first time in my life I felt the petroleum rivers under my feet and they were sloshing.

The horses disappeared on the horizon, but returned when the sun set. They haven't left my side since and they both bear the name destiny.

Not that it's any help now. The truth is, broncos don't like elevators and I'm not much for them either, especially stuck like this. All three of us are panicking. A beetle falls from my eye onto my pearl-snap shirt pocket and it reminds me of my Reckoners. I cross-draw two copies of the old-time guides and flip through the burnt pages. Our monster nemesis may have sabotaged this elevator, but I know there will be something in these books to help us. They've never failed us yet.

Sure enough, I find the chart to free us and the horses grunt and clack their hooves while I do mathematical calculations. I finish and show my hot-headed horse where to stomp in the elevator's weak spot. We climb out of the elevator and I turn back to kick it. It doesn't make a dent, but the scuff from my boot gives me satisfaction. The monster's going to have to try harder—

this is the new Western and I refuse to be written off.

The whole downtown shakes as we rumble down the sidewalk. We're late for our showdown, but my horses are fast. When we roar into the shopping mall, the monster's already in the food court waiting for us, sipping a latte and checking his phone.

No one looks up. They don't care that there's a monster in their midst, sitting placid while his enterprises wreak destruction. He probably has machines toppling trees right now. Factories making poisons to snuff out flies with iridescent wings and eyes that hold all the colours of creation. The first time the broncos pointed them out, I wept and the beetles that fell out of my eyes withered from the fumes in their proximity.

We've been chasing the monster for three years. We've had a few scuffles, but he's always steps ahead. My horses showed him to me on the day of their birth and mine. We galloped into the city thinking we'd change everything. There was no smoke in the air and all the poplars along the highway waved and egged us on.

Now I'm losing calcium and my eyes are full of beetles. The monster's older than me, but a picture of youth. People shrink from me, but they can't get enough of him. His face is on the cover of every local magazine. They say he's our city's very own 'hero-entrepreneur' and 'influencer'.

I've caught glimpses of him in old time westerns—he plays landowners and ranchers, laying claim to land that's not his. The name and face varies, but the eyes never change.

Now he trademarks seeds and makes poisons to kill 'weeds'. He's been clearing prairie in all his iterations and he's never stopped hating poplars.

He's diversified his businesses. It's not just land and agriculture—he has part interest in the production of sharp-phones. They're marketed as smart-phones, but more stylish. I know they're something more—those phones can cut to the bone.

Even worse, they limit imagination and warp vision so when people see me, their eyes show them a woman past her prime dragging two leather reins, not a hero with two destinies in the new Western.

Our eyes meet and he takes a last sip of latte and throws the cup on the floor. He takes off his suit jacket and lets it fall on top. He crushes them both with his alligator loafer and a shopper gasps at the sacrifice of something so expensive. He grins—he loves waste more than anything.

Me and my broncos approach and I feel people watching. They can't see the horses, but they feel the rising tension. I hear whispering and people rummaging for their phones. Someone says, "crazy lady." I tighten my jaw and resolve not to listen.

I lift my chin and try to straighten my spine. The monster shakes his head as though he pities me. The crowd titters.

I try to speak, but my tongue twists. My broncos neigh on my behalf. I pull out a Reckoner and aim it. The monster makes a face like he's scared and the crowd laughs even louder. He opens the flap of his bag.

I'm about to throw the Reckoner when a bronco steps in front of me. It's the soft one, the one that's expressive. She blinks and her eyes say we don't need this. My other bronco snorts and looks away.

My horses look the same, but they couldn't be any more different. One is hot-headed and mad at the world, the other's a gentle peace-maker. The angry one wants to fight everything and turn the world upside down, the soft one wants to let the world be. She thinks peace and love will solve everything.

My soft bronco looks to the west and I follow her gaze. Can't see a thing in this food court, but I know what her mind sees: a sky candy-pink from wildfires, a sea of yellow canola, flies buzzing hypnotic, and past that, a refuge of poplars.

I blink to tell her I also see it. I can feel my resolve softening; there's a part of me that knows fighting is futile, especially throwing two beat up books at a monster who's resourced with everything. My back aches, and I wouldn't mind an afternoon in the trees. Though peace can't help us— I've seen enough westerns to know that, at least.

The monster taps his fingers on the bag, mocking me. The crowd thins, tired of waiting. I exhale and feel my adrenaline draining. My knees tremble. I've been standing too long and that elevator took too much out of me. I put my arm out to lean on a column.

My angry bronco huffs, but understands I need rest. The monster says something under his breath and the remaining onlookers break out laughing. A beetle falls from my eye and I step to the side to avoid squishing it. People see an aging woman losing her footing. My horses steady me and somebody giggles. My angry horse snorts, wanting to trample everything. I tell him we'll get revenge another day.

I climb on the horses bareback and we race to the exit. The city shudders under our weight and we can feel the elevators in parkades underground buckling. We race west down the highway and don't slow until we're far from the skyscrapers. I dismount in a field and we wade through waist-high canola. We ignore the 'No Trespassing' sign, and the logo of the monster's trademarked seed. My angry bronco takes out her anger on the canola while my soft bronco and I walk through the crops.

We come to a poplar bluff and lean against the trees. The flies shine technicolour under the afternoon sun. The air is acrid and the smoke's too thick to see the horizon. There are fewer poplars now to slow the wildfires.

I kick off my boots and press my toes into the earth. Can almost feel the petroleum rivers rushing under us. Before the horses, I never felt them. I was a side character in someone else's narrative. There was much in that life that I missed.

I take off my hat and lie back against my broncos. Flies sing and I almost forget about the monster. We relax into each other and when the sun sets, we watch bats fly jagged and listen to coyotes yip under a sky with no moon.

We don't stay long in the poplars. By morning, my angry bronco's bouncing off trees and searching for barbed-wire fences to topple. She wants back to the city to hunt monsters, but by the time we get there, our lungs are sore from the thick smoke. So we lounge on the sofa in our skyscraper rental, the broncos dozing on each side of me while I watch the river reflect pink off the smoke-cloaked sun.

It's hard for the horses in the city. Crowds make them uneasy and they spook at construction and the skyscrapers that pen us in. They hate our 17th-floor apartment—we're on our second warning and this is our fourteenth rental. I'm struggling to pay rent and don't have a source of income. It doesn't matter that I'm fighting a monster or that I can cross-draw my Reckoners like the lightning that made me, no one will give me a job. The landlords in this city don't care about our vocation, they just point to clauses in the rental agreement about cleanliness and noise.

It's easier for the monster. Everything is. It doesn't matter that he razes poplars and poisons insects, or that he warps peoples' minds with those sharp-phones. His pinstripes and wealth give him glamour. Before my rebirth, he would have cowed me. There was a lot that cowed me then.

The air shifts in my rental and the flies in my kitchen stop buzzing. They can sense the vibrations of those alligator loafers on cement. The static noise of all those sharpened cellphones. I don't feel it, but I trust my horses and those flies. It can only mean one thing.

My hard bronco grunts and paws the cushions. My soft bronco looks at me pleading, *no violence*. I hesitate and my hard bronco explodes a cushion. She wants badly to fight. She murders cushions and I pick up batting until finally I give up, reach for my Stetson hat and follow her out the door.

We walk downtown instead of driving and the streets, as always, are empty. We track the monster to the same downtown shopping mall that doubles as an office building. People jostle me on both sides, talking into phones and dragging shopping bags. Someone pushes me from behind. I spin round and reach for my Reckoners—but it's just a shopper encumbered with bags. I put away my books, then I'm hit from the side. This time I turn to face a man with white hair and black eyes.

I expect him to flinch, but instead he leans into me. His eyes widen and he takes in the broncos. "I'm sorry."

I can't speak. It's the first time anyone but a monster has seen the horses. For a moment I freeze, and then I want to say everything. How I was born a second time with lightning. How each bronco bears the name destiny. But my tongue twists and I choke.

My angry bronco pulls me. I turn to calm her and when I look back, the man's gone. I search the crowd but can't find him anywhere. I scan the mall again and my eyes lock on the monster.

His eyes glimmer and he smiles at me. He yanks off his earpiece, then crunches it under his loafer. He spills his latte over it, reveling in the waste.

My angry bronco paws the ground. Our blood rushes in time and I can feel her anger. My soft bronco blinks, but it's too late. I take out my Reckoners as the monster lifts the flap of his bag. He pulls out a sharp-phone and swipes wide. A garbage can flies and chicken bones and soiled napkins splatter shoppers. My broncos take off, but the monster's too fast. He swings again and a shopping bag shreds. He lifts the sharp-phone a third time.

I'm there a moment later. I slap the monster with each side of a Ready Reckoner while my broncos trample the sharp-phone. Someone yells, "Call security."

By the time they grab my arms and pull me off the monster, the broncos are frothing. Mall security helps the monster to his feet and returns his flattened phone.

The security guards step back when a man in uniform approaches like some old-time sheriff. I take him for police, then realize he's a bylaw officer. He takes out a notepad and looks up and down at me.

I straighten my tongue. "I was fighting the monster."

He raises an eyebrow and looks at the monster. The monster shakes his head and the officer suppresses a smile. "Lady, the world doesn't need heroes like you."

My broncos snort while he writes me a tickets for 'causing disorder' and tells me I'm 'lucky' the monster's not pressing charges. When the bylaw officer and mall security turn to leave, the monster smirks and makes an obscene gesture.

I spend the afternoon waiting in line to pay my fine. The bylaw officer wrote me a note on the back, *you should talk to someone about that temper*. I take a pen to scratch it out, but the words are still legible. When I get to the front to pay, the clerk reads the note and looks at me. I clench my jaw and I can't stop my face from reddening.

We spend the evening watching westerns, they're my broncos' favourite. The broncos doze off and I turn to the news—it's all about the approaching wildfires. I'm about to change the channel when the face of the monster fills up the screen and the news-reader announces a 'leading entrepreneur' has opened a new pesticide plant. At the end of the report she notes the entrepreneur recently endured an 'unprovoked' attack at the mall. I throw a Reckoner at the screen.

The next day me and my angry bronco are hungry for a fight and even my soft bronco doesn't argue with us. We track the monster to a coffee shop. He's in line waiting for a premium ristretto. A sharp-phone sticks out of his bag. The broncos lunge forward, and I fly into a couple in line in front of me. Someone behind me shouts, "Ma'am!"

The monster spins round. His eyes glimmer and he doesn't even show surprise. He lifts a finger to his lips and points across the street: the underground parkade.

I nod and call my horses to my sleeves. The monster takes his ristretto and saunters, sipping, to the street. It kills us to wait, but we've already attracted enough attention. The monster disappears into the parkade, and we step onto the street and follow him. The parkade has six storeys, but we know he'll be on the bottom. We race down the stairs—we're not falling for the elevator trap again.

There are no cars in the lot and there's only one fluorescent flickering. The monster's at the back, leaning against a concrete column. He's taken out his sharp-phone and loosened his tie. He throws his coffee cup to the ground and stomps on his suit jacket. He would waste the whole world if he could. He starts to charge and my horses and I run forward to meet him.

One bronco stomps the monster's hand and the other one kicks his phone. I'm slower, but already aiming my Reckoners. I throw them one-by-one at his face. It feels good, though part of me knows it's futile. The monster pulls a sharp-phone from a hidden pocket and swipes at my bronco. Time slows and I can't breathe. He misses, but my legs are shaking and the next time the monster lunges, it's at me.

This time he doesn't miss. I bring my hand to my cheek and feel blood. He raises his sharp-phone a second time and a bronco slams into him. He cries out and turns to run. My broncos give chase.

They disappear up the stairwell and I try to follow, but they're way ahead of me. When I finally reach the street, it's deserted. I trust my beetles and head for the mall.

It's even more crowded than last time. There's no sign of horse or monster, so I take an escalator up a level and cross the pedway to the office building across the street. I'm almost there when I hear a crash and a neigh. I start to run.

It's the end of the day, so the building lobby is empty. Even the security guards have disappeared on their rounds. I find my broncos and the monster by the elevators. Both broncos are bleeding and the monster's dropped his sharp-phone. My breath catches. This is the first time we've cornered him.

I rush forward as the elevator chimes. The doors open and the man with white hair and black eyes steps outside. He drops his briefcase at the sight of the broncos and our eyes meet a second time.

For a moment, it's just the four of us: me, my two horses and the first person to really see us. I can't breathe. I forget about the monster. I want to tell him everything. His eyes soften, but his expression changes when he sees the monster.

The monster takes us in. He smiles wide and the next moment he's moving so fast even my broncos can't react. I blink and he has the man in a chokehold and the cellphone blade taut on his throat.

I call for help but there's no sign of security. They're never here when it matters, when the monster gives up the facade of upstanding citizen and shows his true face. And of course we're in the one corner of the lobby without any cameras.

I throw my hat to distract the monster and the broncos kick at his phone. The man squirms out of the monster's trip.

"Run!" I yell to him.

My horses rear. The monster flees, and the broncos start after him, but I call them back to my forearms. I'm concerned about the blood. I run my fingers along their backs; they both have gashes but they're shallow. My injury's worse—my face is gushing blood and my cheek hangs loose like a flap.

"Here." The man holds out a handkerchief. His arm is trembling.

I want to say something, but by the time my tongue untwists the words are gone. The man waits and we look at each other. My legs are shaking. I can only stand there and watch while he leaves. He turns back once to look at me and a surge of electricity rises up in my belly and then fades.

Days pass and I'm still thinking about the man from the elevator. It's not just that I saved him. He saw my horses. He gave me a handkerchief.

One night, I dream about it. When I rescue the man from the monster, he mouths to me, *"Thank you."* My tongue is straight and instead of standing there, I tell him everything. We go west of the city and laugh under poplars and I show him how if he puts his feet just so, he can hear the petroleum rivers below. The dream lingers in my mind even upon waking.

We're listless in the city and my broncos won't settle, so I take them out west on the highway. The broncos graze on crops and we trample 'No Trespassing' signs until we reach our poplars.

We wander through the trees and find ourselves in a meadow of willow, dogwood, and wild rose. The land is pink and blooming. The smoky sun makes the colours more vivid. Beetles tumble from my eyes and burrow into the earth while the broncos nibble on flowers. I call my horses by their name and wonder why my own name is lost to me.

It's no secret why I was nameless before. I know how the world sees me. If this were an old-time movie, I wouldn't survive the first scene. But this is the new Western and I'm the main character. I get to choose who to be, even if I need two stubborn broncos to show me the possibilities.

We walk through flowers for hours. Our shadows lengthen and the meadow becomes more spectacular. I wish the man with white hair were here to see it. My eyes linger on the blooms and an idea comes to me.

I'm back at in the shopping mall with a feeling I don't recognize in my belly. My angry bronco's not impressed, she's swishing her tail and glaring at me. The softer one is quiet—she understands that even though I hunt monsters, there's more to me.

I walk through the food court, then browse in the stores. A security guard locks eyes on me and raises a walkie-talkie. When I look again, there are three security guards walking in step behind me. I ignore them and keep going, I'm not here to fight.

I cross two pedways so I'm back in the office tower. Workers rush by with their briefcases and earpieces. The blood by the elevator's been mopped up and there's no sign of our fight. Flies and cockroaches scuttle in the corner, going around their business. I don't see who I'm looking for.

I'm leaving the mall, about to give up when our eyes meet. The man with white hair nods at all three of us and my angry bronco who was swishing her tail and hating the world a moment ago bats her eyes at him and prances.

I wipe a beetle from each eye and try to quiet the flutter in my chest. I step in front of the man and hold out my present. I take a deep breath and force out the words I spent all of last night practicing.

"For you."

There's a pause and he doesn't speak. He hesitates, then leans forward and takes the bouquet. He drops it a moment later.

My stomach sinks and I realize my mistake. These are wild roses; the stems are covered with thorns.

The man pulls out a handkerchief to protect his hand. He picks up the stems and frowns. Mall security crowds around us for a better look.

The hard bronco huffs like I'm stupid. I look to the soft one, but she won't meet my eyes. Too late, I understand—it's not just the thorns, it's that I've handed him stems. Only stems. I've messed up again.

I start to explain how the broncos ate the blooms, but my tongue twists and my voice falters. I can feel myself reddening. I try to speak and beetles free-fall from my eyes. One lands on his tie. He recoils and brings his handkerchief to his mouth like he's going to vomit. I step back, into a guard.

The guard pulls away and makes a face.

The second guard holds up his hands and says, "Stay away!"

My legs are shaking, but I turn and start running anyway. My knees give out after a few steps, so my horses take turns carrying me. We gallop westward and I cry beetles while my cheek flaps in the smoke.

I try to forget the mall, but it eats at me. I can't stand that the monster's out there, clearing land and poisoning insects. My angry bronco wants to hunt and ambush him. She thinks it's a matter of might and getting lucky. We cornered him once, after all.

My soft bronco just blinks. She knows we're unmatched. She thinks we'll prevail through patience, that the monster will see the error of his ways. He just needs someone to show him the beauty of flies' infinite eyes or how poplar leaves shimmer like gold under late afternoon sun.

They're both wrong. I didn't used to dare think it, but we've had too many confrontations for denial. We've taken too many beatings, paid too many tickets, and been expelled from too many malls. He's not even fazed by our fights. Once he told me he was 'humouring me' by letting us chase him. He said that I should thank him. I hate that he's right.

We're bored in the rental, but the smoke makes us sluggish. We watch the smoke thicken above the river and when it gets dark we turn to Netflix. The broncos want watch westerns but I'm sick of the genre. I want to try something different. I watch a rom-com and then another. There's something comforting about the genre. The plots are the same in both movies: the main characters start plain and unhappy. They face obstacles, but solve them through makeovers, book clubs, and meeting someone new. No one gets hurt, and nothing's at stake. By the end of both movies, the main characters are pretty, happy, and loved.

I'd like that. To be welcomed by security guards instead of followed by them. I stand in the mirror and try to picture it. Touch my hand to the wound on my cheek and wipe a shiny beetle from my eye. If I were in a rom-com, I'd know to give someone I just met thornless cultivated roses, not the thorny stems from wild bronco-eaten blooms.

It's not easy to find a book club that's taking new members. I drive deep into the suburbs for my first meeting, wearing long sleeves to hide my broncos and making the flies in the car nervous with my jitters.

I ring the bell, and when the host opens the door her eyes widen. She recovers, then lets me inside.

The other members have manicured nails and matching lip gloss. I shake hands with stiff arms, hoping my broncos won't act up. The book club members ask if I'm married and where I went to school. I study the floor. They ask about family and I tell them I once had a dog named Gambler—my bronco snorts at the lie. They ask about kids and I mention the early menopause. They say they're sorry and I tell them I've never felt so alive.

We discuss a book that sounds like a rom-com and eat delicate canapes. The host passes out Prosecco in crystal flutes. We lean over the coffee table decorated with gold-brushed pinecones and vanilla-scented candles. I start to feel hope. When we clink glasses, I laugh for the first time in both my lives.

Somehow I volunteer to host the next meeting. The other members look worried, but the host reassures me. She walks me to the door and says I did 'great'. I blush and look away, but by the time I reach my car I'm beaming.

I sing to my flies all the drive home. My broncos snore the whole way, still behaving. There's something strange and lovely rising in my belly. It feels good to be a book club member. Maybe if I keep going to the meetings, I'll stop shedding beetles.

Back in my apartment, I open my closet and look for something other than cowboy clothes. I put on red lipstick and imagine myself with matching nails. I stand in the mirror with a bronco over each of my shoulders. My angry bronco snorts, disgusted, and my soft bronco blinks. For the first time ever, I can't read her eyes.

I pick up the book club paperback, but can't get into it. Read three more pages, then rip out the spine. The sound pleases me. I look up and both broncos are staring. My face reddens, but my hard bronco neighs. For once she approves.

I rummage for tape to repair the book, but my apartment's a mess. How will I ever host a bookclub? The living room's full of batting from smashed cushions and the coffee table is in two pieces. Swarms of flies live in my kitchen. I have no bowls of pinecones or scented candles to create mood. No sparkling wine or crystal flutes.

I call the horses to my sleeves and head out for the drugstore. When I come back to the apartment, I'm $25 dollars poorer and have a package of metal instruments. I can't afford it, but I know this is important. Spend two hours in the bathroom working on my fingers. I mangle my thumb, but by the end of it my brittle nails are painted crimson like blood.

The manicure takes everything out of me. I collapse on the sofa between my broncos. They put their heads on my shoulders and sniff my now-foreign fingers. I stroke their manes and tell them there are horses in rom-coms too. My angry bronco snorts and turns away.

My gentle bronco watches me. I know what her eyes say: we don't have to choose between book clubs and monsters. That we can stay here, just us three, watching the river. Or go west and wander through farmers' fields, communing with flies, rolling in monocultures and creating new spaces in the landscape for new poplars and wild roses to grow.

The river shines pink and the wildfire smoke makes me sleepy. I'm just starting to doze when my angry bronco leaps onto the sofa and cracks the frame. Her eyes are wild. The flies in my kitchen stop buzzing and we all know the monster's nearby.

My angry bronco slams herself against the front door. My heart is racing in time with her frenzy, but I fumble the lock, so she throws herself at the door frame, cracking it. *There's our third warning.* She shoots down the stairwell, no patience for elevators.

I put on my boots and reach for my hat. My soft bronco blinks with sad eyes. I tell her she can stay, but when I start down the hall her hooves clack on the linoleum behind me. Her eyes are hopeful all the way down the elevator. She doesn't want to fight, but she'll come with me.

We track the monster into the city centre, darting between buildings and empty streets. We rush through the mall so the security guards won't see us on our way to the office tower. There's a security guard at the elevator and another at the front desk. I hide my face and try to muffle the sound of my boots. I can't help the sound of the hooves on the marble.

We inch along the lobby, skulking behind mirrored columns and giant planters, and leaving a trail of beetles. When we come to the stairwell, we sniff the air. The broncos meet my eye and all the bugs in the corners confirm our suspicions. We race down the stairs to the parkade.

There's a thick metal door at the bottom level. I need both hands to wrest it open. It slams closed at our back. There's not a car in the lot and only one fluorescent light. The monster's slouching in a corner with a latte. He leers when he sees me and pats his bag with the sharp-phones. My angry bronco snorts.

The monster throws his cup so hard the sound echoes. He takes out a sharp-phone and holds it above his head. We don't breathe and for a moment there's no sound. Then the monster speaks.

"You can't possibly win. Why don't you just give up?"

I hesitate. We've had this conversation before. I can't bear that the monster speaks truth.

My hard bronco snorts and waits for me to signal attack. Seconds pass and I'm still standing there. The monster's right, this is futile. But I can't give up on my broncos—it would kill them if they knew. They each have hope, in their own way.

Besides, what else can I do? The other book club members don't even like me. The host is nice, but that's probably politeness. I'll never be pretty like in the rom-coms. And I'm not going back to my old life—it wasn't just the dog I lied about at the book club meeting.

My hard bronco snorts and rears on her hind legs. My soft bronco's eyes plead. I sigh and give the sign.

My hard bronco charges and I follow her with the Reckoners. The monster side-steps my horse and ends up behind me. He lunges with his sharp-phone—I try to dodge, but I'm too slow. Feel a hot pinch on my arm and another, hotter behind my elbow. I jump backwards, drop my Reckoners. Blood squirts onto my shirt. The monster raises his sharp-phone again.

I throw my head forward and head-butt him. My beetles fly into his eyes and he staggers backward blinded. Tries to stab me with his phone, but he's not even close. He doesn't see when my angry bronco kicks, aiming her hooves at his knees.

A moment later he's on the ground knee-capped. His face is purple and he's hugging his legs. This is the first time we've got him on the ground. My angry bronco neighs and prances—she thinks we've won. I almost dare to believe it.

I look down at the monster and have no idea what to do next. He's still groaning and not getting up, so I call my horses and lead them away. I'm just about to open that heavy door when the monster rushes us from behind with the biggest sharp-phone I've ever seen.

There's no time to react. He leaps toward me and I turn and crash headfirst into the metal door. My ears ring and the world becomes bright lights. There's a gust of air as the monster wields his sharp-phone and I brace for the inevitable impalement.

Instead there's a neigh and a loud thud. My vision clears and the monster's on the ground, dazed by the bronco that toppled him. My hard bronco shrieks and I lunge for her bridle to keep her from trampling his face. She makes a sound I've never heard and strains against me.

Somewhere to the side, there's a whimper. *No—my soft bronco.* Then I feel it in my viscera, the only good part of me, my heart, my world, ripping apart.

My bronco's on her side and I can barely see the giant sharp-phone, it's so deeply wedged. Her chest cavity is open wide, exposing slashed muscle and ribs that shine moon-white. She looks at me anguished and I can't meet her eyes. I fall to my knees.

It's my fault. I should have known he couldn't let us beat him. For all his talk about us being mere irritants, his world doesn't have space for roses or poplars. He despises flies and broncos named destiny with big hopeful eyes. It's not just the land he wants to burn and make all the same, he won't even abide dreams of other possibilities.

I touch my arm to her side, but she's too weak to climb into it. The cement behind us is splattered crimson and when I raise my arm it's dripping blood too.

My angry bronco screams and stomps so hard the cement shatters. The monsters flinches when we turn to him. I close my hands into fists and throw myself at his face. My bronco stomps on his hands. He curls up into a ball and moans. When we're done, he doesn't look like a monster. He doesn't look like anything.

The blood around my bronco submerges my Reckoners. I scoop them up and flip through the pages, but there's no chart or calculation that can help her. I rip the pages to make a bandage, but it has no effect. I rip their spines and throw them away from me.

My angry bronco kicks cement columns until they buckle. The whole ceiling heaves. I kneel down beside my injured bronco. She rasps while she breathes. Salty beetles fall from my eyes and drown in her crimson sea.

We can barely open the metal door and carry my injured bronco up the stairs. It's my angry bronco that bears her. We leave a blood trail when we leave and we don't look back at the crumpled monster.

The vets turn us away, saying there's nothing they can do. It doesn't help that they can't see the horse, or that my other bronco is stomping the ground and snorting at them. They call it harassment and threaten to call the police on me.

We leave smears of blood on the elevator and down the hall to our apartment. My injured bronco survives the night, but doesn't improve the next day. She lies on the exploded cushions on my sofa breathing too fast, lips ashen. My other bronco's beside herself, destroying the cupboards and then the bed frame.

We watch the news and the announcement about the monster retiring from business after a 'freak attack and injury'. A policeman who looks like a sheriff says they're investigating. My angry bronco snorts at the television, but her heart's not in it. The victory's cost too much.

Two days after the fight, my angry bronco starts on the windows and I get an eviction notice the same day. After three days, the other bronco's barely moving. I don't know if she sees the smoky skies or the pink-reflecting river, or if she notices the thick smoke that wafts in through our shattered windows.

On the fourth day after the fight, I decide fresh air and trampling is worth a try. We drive west and I point the broncos to a field. My hard-headed horse goes through the motions, but doesn't take her eyes off her partner. My injured bronco lies unmoving on the canola. Her wound is full of flies and she stains the yellow crops red.

I take off my boots and sit with her. Press my toes into the ground, but the earth is compacted. I bend down to put my ear to the ground, but I can't hear the petroleum river. I listen for flies, but they're drowned out by the bronco's rasping. When dusk comes, the coyotes are silent and the smoke's too thick for bats to fly.

We return to the apartment, and the broncos collapse on the sofa. The hurt one is breathing so loudly that the kitchen chairs and the broken windows are rattling. I put my hand on her mane and her eyes almost focus on me. The other bronco pauses from destroying the television. I can't look at either of them.

I thought the new Western meant possibility, but now my future is withering right in front of me. We had a dream of space for poplars. I let out a sob and beetles gush from my eyes.

It's hard to think with the rasping and with both broncos watching me. More beetles fall and I think of the mall. When I leave the apartment, my arms are bare. I don't even bring my Stetson.

It's strange in the elevator without the broncos and I enter the mall feeling naked. The horses have become a part of me, I haven't been alone in years.

We pass a news crew and I stop to see someone interviewing a new 'hero-entrepreneur'. He tells the interviewer he just moved to town and he has big plans for the city and surrounding area. His face is different and he's taller. He makes herbicides not pesticides and his monoculture of choice is wheat. Instead of sharp-phones, he makes razor-wearables.

Our eyes meet and he pauses his speech. He smirks, but it's so fleeting the interviewer misses it. His eyes glimmer and he's speaking to me and praising the unstoppable spirit of industry.

I pass a mirror and recoil: my jeans are ripped and bloody, and one of my boots is missing a heel. The flap from my slashed cheek has fallen away, leaving a hollow. The only pretty part of me is the crushed beetle on my temple.

The mall is crowded, but the shoppers give me wide berth. I walk with my head down so mall security won't see me. Almost walk into a little girl dragging a giant shopping bag. I smile when she looks up, but her eyes widen and she calls her mom.

Her mom has nails like she belongs to a book club. I hold out my hand so she'll see I'm a book club member too, but the movement makes the little girl jump. She opens her mouth and screams, "Monster!"

That gets mall security's attention. One of the guards raises his walkie-talkie and the other motions with his hand. I prepare for confrontation, but both guards take two steps back, grimacing and making way.

The new monster pauses another interview to shake his head and wag his finger at me.

I find a drugstore that sells bandages and keep my eyes down at the cash. I lose a beetle while I'm paying and the cashier gasps.

When I reach the exit, the man with white hair is standing by the door. I look away, I can't take another humiliation, but it's too late, he sees me and calls out as I pass.

My face gets hot but I don't slow.

He starts after me. "I'm sorry!"

My throat catches. I take a step, then hesitate. My hot-headed bronco wouldn't waste time on something so frivolous, she'd be charging the new monster in the mall. But the peace-maker...I know what she'd do.

I start to turn. Have a vision of my soft bronco blinking. She'd want me to be kind. To have hope. She always saw so many possibilities. Like wandering through wild roses and making space for poplars. Holding hands and yipping with coyotes, then watching bats under the moon.

I straighten my tongue, but before I speak that image from the parkade comes back to me and the grief makes me choke.

His face falls and something inside me crashes. I push down the surge of feelings.

He apologizes a second time, but I'm already leaving.

I reach my building and step into the elevator. My eyes are overflowing with beetles and my bronco's blood is still smeared on the mirror.

I let out a sigh and my shoulders deflate. This isn't how I imagined the story. There's a mad bronco trashing my apartment and another on my sofa that's barely alive. Wildfires will reach the city any day. There are 'No Trespassing' signs and lonely bluffs of poplars to the west waiting for me. A monster I can never defeat. We'll be evicted on the weekend and tomorrow I'm hosting a book club. I haven't figured out anything.

I may or may not have a destiny. I still don't have a name. This is the new Western and it's being rewritten in this moment. I study my reflection and consider who I'll be.

See E.C. Dorgan's story "The New Western" online at Metaphorosis.
If you liked it, leave a comment. Authors love that!
Remember to subscribe to our e-mail updates so you'll know when new stories are posted.

About the story

I had an image of this character standing in a bright yellow canola field in a lightning storm while two broncos galloped off her forearms. I was simultaneously thinking about how there aren't a lot of "coming-of-age" stories with older characters. I became increasingly curious about this character, and I wanted her to have agency and a say in where her story took her. I didn't want the story to be neat and tidy. I also wanted it to have action, since most of my stories are slower. As I wrote the story, the broncos took on a life of their own. The hardest part in writing this story was figuring out how the broncos interacted with the world around them. I couldn't resist adding insects to the mix since they're quite beautiful and amazing and they often don't get credit.

A question for the author

Q: Do you often include animals in your stories? What role do they play?

A: Animals seem to turn up in my stories—while I don't consciously decide to include them, I would say that most of my stories have animals in them. I'm not a big plotter and I tend to write stories based on strong images. Often I will get pre-occupied with an image of a particular animal if I see one in my regular life. Lately I've had a bit of a horse fascination, though I don't see those often. My characters often have relationships with animals, either cats or dogs, or as in this latest story, broncos and insects. These relationships help to "show" characters, but I also just really like writing about them.

About the author

E.C. Dorgan writes dark fiction and monster stories on Treaty 6 territory in Alberta, Canada. She has a soft spot for poplars and insects and is not fond of rom-coms.

A word about Damien Krsteski

Damien Krsteski's first story for us was "Lake Oreyd", in the March 2017 issue of Metaphorosis. I loved it's strange world of snail-shaped churches on the edge of a lake (and was happy to have recognized its origin in Macedonia's similarly church-studded Lake Ohrid).

His story "One of the Cities" appeared in our *Reading 5X5* anthology in 2018, and the post-apocalyptic "The Trader" was in the emotionally-ordered *Score* anthology in 2019.

We were happy to have Damien's work back in Metaphorosis again with "Esma's Margaret", an emotive story of hackers and automated therapy in January 2021. That broad concept arises again in the next story, "Core", though in an entirely different way.

Core

Damien Krsteski

1.

Walking up to the door, I grabbed Ellie's hand and subvocalized, *You got this.*

"I know," she snapped. "I'm completely fine."

So be it, I thought, and squeezed her hand.

The door swung open and Mr. Mueller beamed at us. "Right on time, ladies."

He ushered us into the living room and poured the three of us a warm cup of valerian brew. I hated the stinky stuff, but the Muellers had elevated its consumption to a family tradition, so like it or not, I was destined to drink this disgusting cat-piss until the end of my days. (I'd refused when Ellie brewed it at home, but here, as a guest in the Mueller house, I didn't dare voice my taste—or hepatotoxicity—concerns, certainly not today of all days, so I sipped as little as possible and smiled.)

"How's work, Alice?" he asked me. "Your company was in the feeds again."

"It's been busy," I said, playing down the chaos in which we'd collectively embroiled ourselves recently. Training AIs to perform therapy for overseas patients carried risks; especially if those foreign hospitals our company targeted could afford only the cheapest of licenses for our software, then stretched the terms of use to their legal and practical limits by recycling the same AI agent for multiple patients. Which in turn caused confusion, ineffective treatments, and in several extreme cases, worsening of symptoms leading to fatalities. Obviously, our company and product were blanketed in layers of legalese, so we were deemed safe come litigation or audit, but the press that followed the incidents was in no way good for our business. Public consensus was that it remained our company's duty to make sure our products were used to spec.

"No doubt. Just the other day I was reading reports about this clinic in Bolivia, where one of your—what do you call them, digital therapists?—got so clogged up with patient information that it started spewing entire sessions back at them, giving advice on claustrophobia to a schizophrenic, and treating a narcissistic person for alcoholism. Ridiculous."

Mr. Mueller was an educated man, albeit not a scientist; even so, he enjoyed teasing me for my chosen profession. I always took his jabs in stride, writing them off as the unavoidable bickering of in-laws which had plagued marriages since time immemorial, and I tended to respond in kind. Tonight, though, considering what was about to come, I decided to let him have this one win. I resigned, saying, "A failure on our part. We should have foreseen this and implemented better safety checks."

"Yes," he said, looking slightly disappointed, as if just deprived of a juicy debate. "Safety checks, remote monitoring, circuit-breakers, yes, yes."

The discussion then veered toward Ellie and her latest project, and Mr. Mueller simply nodded politely as he always did when she talked about her art. We sipped our tea. We nibbled on cashews and peanuts. When our stomachs began to rumble, Mr. Mueller carried the valerian tea tray away and brought out a spinach quiche and a bottle of cider.

I finished my piece and had helped myself to a second serving when Mr. Mueller realized Ellie hadn't touched her slice. He said, "Is everything okay, dear?"

"We're going to have a baby," Ellie said.

Mr. Mueller stared at us for a moment and said, "Well, that's fantastic news." He laughed. "I'll go fetch the real stuff." He stood up, but before he could disappear down into the cellar, I nudged my wife.

"Planning to," she said. "We're not pregnant yet. We're just planning to."

"Still," he said after a beat. "That's news worth celebrating."

"You didn't ask us how."

"What do you mean how? Splice, obviously." He pointed at the two of us and mimed the exchange of genetic material by waving his hands from Ellie to me and back. "Or, are you thinking of going for a male donor? A friend? A colleague?" This last question directed at me, as if Ellie couldn't possibly have any male colleagues at the art institute of *good stock*.

"No, dad," she said. "None of those, really."

"Oh." His smile slipped from his face. He sat back down. "Then what?" But he knew, and his eyes showed it. He was a man who followed the feeds, and we'd discussed this latest trend before, or, as he'd referred to it, *latest cult*, and he quickly put two and two together. After a while, he said, "So that's why you're here, then? To duly inform me my grandchild will be a *world-baby*? A step-child of globalism? An orphan with millions of parents?"

I could sense Ellie pulling back, so I interrupted: "Mr. Mueller, please. There's no need for this. We already—"

"Don't." He raised a hand to stop me.

Softly, I said, "You haven't had any time to process."

"This is bullshit."

"I believe it's best we leave you to it."

I stood up and tugged at Ellie. We dressed, and we were on our way out when she turned. "You know, Dad," she said, "an orphan with millions of parents, loving her each one bit, is still better than the daughter of a man who's head is stuck so far up his own ass he can't tell up from down, right from wrong."

Mr. Mueller opened his mouth to respond, but I said, "That's enough, both of you." He nodded, went back in, and we caught the first bus back home.

2.

Just as I'd expected, Ellie didn't take her father's reaction lightly. She barely slept that night, tossing in bed and keeping me awake too, until we both decided to give up on the preposterous notion of a good night's sleep, and trundled grudgingly down to the kitchen to have a cup or two of espresso before dawn. She complained to me with tears in her eyes, and I just stroked her hand. We'd known he'd react badly, and we'd spoken about it at length beforehand, so in some ways I felt Ellie was exaggerating, playing out a role she'd rehearsed in her head ever since we'd made the decision to have this baby. The hurt daughter. The slighted queen.

Of course, I didn't tell her that.

At the office, I buried myself in work.

Groggy and sleep-deprived, I slipped on my headset, and the panels flooded my retinas with cold light.

In a garden dotted with ponds, I sat at a wooden table opposite a neatly-dressed man: the avatar of one of our CBT software agents. A glance at my wrist display revealed my role was that of an obsessive-compulsive.

The agent began with the usual opening: did I have anything urgent to discuss this session? How had I been coping? Had I been a good patient and done my homework, journaling every clinch of my obsession and each release of the ensuing compulsion? We did the standard warmup Q&A dance, and after ten minutes of that the session properly started.

He asked me if I'd eaten out in town since last we'd spoken, referring to a particularly strong paranoid obsession of the person I was playing: fear of food poisoning from any meal not cooked at home under pristine conditions.

Yes, I subvocalized, *I ate a slice of pizza from this place close to work.* The agents were capable of hearing speech, obviously, but when training them in VR I tended to feel too self-conscious and even a tad insulting, pretending to have a different mental affliction every session, so I preferred to *sub*. I'd let the shirt collar sensors pick up on the electrical storm raised by my neck muscles and convert that thundering to voice, which was in turn relayed straight to the agent's language processing modules.

"Could you describe the experience?" he said.

So I did, inventing as much detail as I could in an attempt to overwhelm the agent with data: the crowd at the restaurant, the color of the napkins, the name of the waiter, the way he touched money before handling my cutlery, my quote-unquote astute observations of the kitchen and its cleanliness from the vantage point of the table by the milkshake machine. And on and on. Let him sort it out, I thought. Figure out what was relevant.

Which, I was surprised to find, he did quite well. He filtered out all the cosmetic details and went straight to the point: what made me think it was *bad* to not wash one's hands a thousand times a day? How dirty could money really be? What made me believe a kitchen had to be absolutely pristine?

Isn't it obvious? I asked.

"No," he responded. "It isn't."

Well okay, I said. *Imagine a flood of bacteria and viruses moving from hand to hand. To my food. Invading my body. Isn't that horrible?*

"Not necessarily. You seem to harbor a deeply ingrained bias. Not all bacteria are harmful. And being exposed to the bacteria or viruses that may be somewhat detrimental to health isn't necessarily a bad thing. In fact, exposure helps us develop immunity, and medical research has repeatedly shown—"

I liked where the agent was taking this conversation, which is why I decided to throw a wrench in his gears.

Why should I care about supposed research?

"Because it is true. The scientific method—"

From the same people who made these viruses, who poisoned our waters.

"Another bias," the agent exclaimed. "The scientific method relies on experimentation, and proof, and replication of results."

Speaking of which, is this an appeal to authority I am hearing?

At which point he launched into a tirade against me, and no matter how much I tried to steer him back on track, the conversational path he'd decided to go down branched out only to confrontational nodes, and to a potential real patient storming out in anger in some clinic somewhere in the world, and to Mr. Mueller catching the exaggerated clickbait about it online and cackling to himself about our poor work or bad auditing or some such.

I realized I was getting all worked up.

Stop, I subvocalized, for the agent's sake as much as mine. *Listen to me now.* Which flipped the switch to learning mode. I explained that he should under no circumstance turn against the patient in such a manner, that he should focus on strategies that involved the patient, cooperated with the patient, walked the patient step-by-step through a novel way of thinking until at long last a cognitive change was triggered. We repeated the sentences. We practiced a few different conversational flows. *Begin again.*

"Why do you consider it bad, not to wash one's hands so often?"

And we went down the same path again, and I pushed and tugged and drove the agent into a corner until he, once more, resorted to attacking.

"No, no, no!" I said out loud and shook my head. Marsha Linehan, this agent wasn't. I scribbled notes in my virtual pad and logged out in frustration.

When I took off my headset, I was surprised to see Phillip standing by my desk.

"That bad, huh?"

"I swear, they get dumber by the session."

"Seems like you're in dire need of a change."

"Of career." I placed the headset on its dock. The panels briefly flashed acid green as it began to charge.

"How about just a change of department to begin with?" An intricate graphic played out on the tablet he held out before me: a stylized human brain, enveloped in a mesh of sorts, with patterns of neuronal firings flashing with varying intensity. When he saw my puzzled expression, Phillip added, "We've been working on a little something for the past year, Alice. You're one of our best trainers here. I want you to see this."

At home things seemed unchanged.

Against my advice, Ellie had called her father during the day, and as expected it had turned ugly real fast. By the end, they'd been shouting at each other, and as was always the case in these bouts of frustration between the two of them, somehow somebody had brought up the topic of her deceased mother. After that prying of open old wounds, all hope of reconciliation would have to be delayed by another two weeks, at the very least. When Ellie finished recounting their argument to me for the second time, she looked up expectantly.

"You have to let him cool off." I lay on the couch and flicked a random feed address at the screen before us. An old movie I'd seen once on an airplane was playing on this feed. "Just drop it. Give him a week. Come, sit."

But she just stared at me, subbed, *You don't get it, do you?* and she lay down beside me theatrically, like a third rate performance of Juliette in Act 5.

3.

To ease her mind, I'd promised Ellie I'd talk to her father myself, so before work I swung by his workplace.

Mr. Mueller had once been a decent network engineer—a chapter of his biography he never failed to bring up—but with the onrush of automation and self-improving software agents of all sorts, human supervision became increasingly redundant: machines had learned to load-balance their own network traffic and to set up their own development infrastructure. ("Look ma, no sysops," as Mr. Mueller liked to put it.) So nowadays, he was a freelance consultant for companies still clinging to the old model of work, or whose software relied on antiquated network architectures which the machines had deemed not worth bothering to master.

I rang the doorbell. For a moment, I thought he wouldn't let me in, but then the latch clicked and the door swung open.

He went back in and slumped in his big chair. "What do you want, Alice?" He swiped a finger over his tablet screen lazily, scrolling through some schematics.

"For you to sober up," I said, "for your daughter's sake."

"Please."

"You two are beyond childish. She, with her stubbornness, and you with your refusal to take a moment to *understand*."

He tucked the tablet between the cushion and armrest and steepled his fingers. "Understand what? That my only daughter refuses to have a normal child? That she's more interested in some philosophical roll of the dice?"

"A *normal* child? With all due respect, Mr. Mueller, but your reaction is just the selfish gene talking. What if we'd opted for adoption?"

"That would be fantastic. Why don't you?"

"It's perfectly within our rights not to justify our choices to you. What is within yours, is either to accept them or not, nothing more. Whether we adopt, have a biological child, or a Child of the World— the decision is ours alone."

"Eyes from Laos, skin tone from Cameroon, mood predispositions or proclivities for music or love of science or literature or even tolerance for goddam milk sugars from the four sides of the globe. You'll be cherry-picking your child's features from a field as wide as the Earth, and I just have to accept, and demand nothing else from you."

Poetic in a feeble effort at ridicule, nonetheless his argument rang hollow. The whole point of having a Child of the World was *not* to cherry-pick, *not* to choose, unlike what most would-be parents did nowadays: selecting their children's looks and faculties from a catalogue in a geneticist's waiting room. First I thought I should let this misunderstanding slide, but I realized that if he were to eventually understand us and our choice, he should have the facts straight.

"The opposite, Mr. Mueller. We don't choose anything. We simply take it all. We take everything this beautiful Earth can give us." I tapped my chest. "What is mine? What comes from me? This body, these cells, these atoms, these ideas? You don't seem to understand that everything is everybody's. And the sooner we all grapple with that fact, the easier the Transition will be."

"The *Transition?*" He studied me awhile, then said, "Those are Ellie's words coming out of your mouth, Alice."

Somehow, this hurt me more than it should have.

"We're both equally onboard. We both want this Child."

"Please," he said. "You don't want a baby," he said. "You want an exercise in combinatorics."

Phillip had me transferred to his department within a couple of days; they were in need of people, fast. With all the commotion around our failed licensing agreements in Latin America, it seemed the company was eager to move at least some of its eggs to a different basket.

"Reprogramming humans," was how he'd originally explained his team's work to me. "Rebuilding memory. Ripping out fear, physically."

"As opposed to?"

"Merely treating it." He winked. "Treating it with *speech*." He mimed gagging.

He showed me around their offices briefly, where in place of headsets on docks and cliché Freudian couches, there were people in lab-coats shuffling about with beakers and pipettes and peering down microscopes. Past them, we went into a meeting room where my official onboarding took place.

I learned, from presentations by young neurologists, all the intricacies of the department's work: the fishnet mesh of microscopic neurobots which glommed onto the brain's topmost layers to observe and direct; the even smaller bots which burrowed their way deeper into the subject's cortex and modulated synaptic activity while scanning the amygdala's responses, closing a real-time feedback loop; the research into the delta opioid receptor agonists that apparently had laid the foundation on which the rest of the work was built. The neurobots, I learned, camped out in their synaptic valleys and meted out these new synthetic chemicals to patients, softening their fear responses, but also helping their brains unlearn the context in which these fears occurred.

"So," I said at the end of one presentation, "the patients start to unlearn their fears, their feelings."

"After one session," the neurologist said.

"Like a sped-up exposure," I said.

"Yes, and no," she said, waved the slides away so a new batch could take their place, "Because we've discovered something altogether different than mere fear eradication. We've realized that patients can shape their opinions, their beliefs. We found that our swarm of neurobots, when directed properly, can work in concert to challenge people's core beliefs. What we've found is a way to *actually* change people's minds."

Inside of a week, I already felt right at home in this department. Work was all-consuming, and the novelty of this research was refreshing to the point where it felt like working in a completely different field.

I was burning through transcripts and video snippets of subjects who'd gone through these therapies and new neurobot hardware, which I learned they affectionately called *the rice*, and had come out with their fears of heights or cats or dogs or abusive lovers fully shed, reemerging as new persons. I played with snapshots of the agents that had guided these patients through their sessions, and started tweaking them somewhat.

Once I finished with the initial batch of recordings, I moved to more intricate subjects, namely people who had come to have what they considered a *bad idea* eradicated. I was significantly more queasy watching people unlearn opinions than basic fears, but I was nonetheless fascinated.

The first case I worked on was a woman who'd lived a sheltered life, and had grown up with an ingrained and burning jealousy of her own sibling, and now that she'd long moved away from home, she knew these feelings were wrong, she knew her envious thoughts were irrational and were keeping her from being close to her family and stunting her other relationships, but nevertheless she couldn't help herself thinking them.

It took her only one session to unlearn. She'd ingested the preprogrammed rice, which had promptly made its way to the brain. It softened her neural tissue, rendering it malleable, and pulsing within her brain the rice made her unlearn, made her change. After the session, she slipped on a headset and dove into soothing scenes where one of our AI agents sat waiting, gently guiding her out of the experience. The following two sessions she had with our agents were mere formality, a debriefing, there to waste everyone's time and to cover our own ass for liability.

So it was with most other cases. People's brains changed or healed on their own and our therapists were just there as a safety net in case the neural hardware had prodded at something that should've stayed untouched. By and large, they remained a formality. Our agents took their notes and nodded at the newly 'healthy' people and the people never requested to speak to them again.

My job was to handle the software agents afterwards and provide feedback, fine-tuning the underlying model, nudging it in the direction of a well-rounded cognitive behavioral therapist.

How do you think that one went? In our pristine immersive environment, just me and this one agent, sitting cross-legged on a generic meadow.

"She seemed relieved." The agent cocked her head. "I don't understand. It was all very fast."

Yes. Very.

"I believe she won't be coming back."

I believe so too.

Before we logged out, the agent said, "One thing might be of note, doctor. I noticed she wasn't feeling any of those 'undesirable' feelings, and she seemed overjoyed, but I was able to sense a layer of discomfort, too, a sort of disorientation. Like she was made a different person all too suddenly. I'm not sure she liked that too much."

4.

The clinic's windows were tinted, but if you looked closely you could still see, meshing with our own shaded reflections, a smattering of protesters on the curb. Brandishing placards that misquoted Crick or Pauling, mutely opening and closing their mouths in unison.

"The ova are almost ready," our doctor said, and Ellie squeezed my hand, which made me turn my attention back to the screen.

On it, countless sprites of four colors shuffled and reshuffled themselves like one of those old screen-savers I'd seen in documentaries. Ellie, who'd chosen to carry our child, stared at this display mesmerized. The graphic represented genes from millions of humans, spliced together base pair by base pair into one coherent genome to produce one baby, one human being. Out of the many, one. It didn't matter who brought which gene to the table, as this was no longer a monogenic, or even a polygenic world. Life was more complex than that, with every single part of the whole contributing in its own way to the final product in an *omnigenic* dance of information playing out in each cell of every human on the planet. And putting it all together, as we were, to bring such a human to life showed we were all just tiny parts of a large singular whole, drops of water at the crest of the same wave.

The doctor gave us some more information and instructions on how to prepare Ellie's body for the implantation to come, then we thanked her profusely, and left out the back door to grab lunch.

The day was mild, the sky bright blue. I saw my drained face reflected in Ellie's sunshades.

"I don't know what to feel," she said, playing with an olive on her plate. "Excitement? Fear? Anxiety?"

"How about you don't try to know, and just feel what you feel, and tell me."

She skewered the olive with her fork, brought it up before her eyes as if for inspection, then popped it in her mouth. "Don't get all professional on me, Al." She chewed, swallowed. "Read the room. I feel all of the fucking above."

"Don't take it out on me."

"Yeah, well," she started, then pursed her lips.

"Well what?"

"Well, why don't you tell me how *you* feel?"

"What's that supposed to mean?"

"About all this."

"What about it? What do you mean?"

"I mean, I know you. I saw your face in there."

"What are you on about?" I said. "I made no face."

"That's right," she said, "you didn't."

We finished the remainder of our lunch in silence.

A chirp came from my office door.

I took off my headset and placed it lenses-up on the table. *Open*, I subvocalized.

Phillip walked in. "Interrupting?"

"I was just finishing up with an agent."

He came up to the headset and peered over it as if to get a glimpse of the scene where I'd been moments before, and the light from the panels lit his face from the chin up. He looked at me, eyes wide, "Wanna hear a scary story?"

"Coffee, Phillip?" I gestured at my espresso machine.

"Let's go for a walk."

We strolled around campus, and he grilled me about the technology, about the trials. "How do you find it?"

"Surprising," I said. "Exciting," I said, surprising myself.

"And how do they find it?" Meaning the agents, the post-procedure specialists meant to gently lull our patients back into polite society.

"They find it equally surprising."

He put a hand on my shoulder. "Let's make it easier for them." A lot depended on them, and he didn't have to say it.

The agents were the link between brain surgery and couch therapy. They were a softener, both for the patients themselves and for any would-be regulators of our technology. As with any other big bio- or neuro-technological product, heavy regulatory oversight was expected for our post-trial rollout, and having agents at the ready was our company's strategy to assuage any overzealous regulators by saying, here's a scalable solution to help people make sense of what they've gone through, holding their hand along the way.

"They've been trained on tons of traditional therapy data," I said. "Which as you know hasn't always been very favorable to any 'biological' solution."

"Yes, yes, do your breathing exercises, don't just take a pill." He pointed to a bench under a tree and we sat down. "We have to improve that."

"I'm on it."

"You have to reinforce different feedback loops."

I nodded, understanding my assignment.

He said, "We need to get them ready."

Later, back in my office, I picked up the headset and held it with the tips of my fingers. It flickered with any slight movement, unsure whether to wake up from its digital sleep. I was already late for our dinner with Ellie. I sent her a message, saying I was stuck in a meeting, and I slipped on the headset to continue working.

That night, Ellie wasn't home.

It worried me, not because of where she could've gone, which I knew exactly, since she always tended to go there whenever we'd have a big fight and always returned the following morning, but because she wasn't home tonight and we'd never even gotten to argue. There was no explosion, no release, just me coming in to an empty home.

All of the trademarked Mueller-versus-Mueller drama was obviously beginning to spill over into our relationship, and it kept eating at me intensely, until one afternoon at work a thought popped into my mind.

I debated with myself for a couple of days, chewing over the bizarre idea in my mind before sleep, until the home mood dropped to an absolute all-time low and I decided that enough was enough for everyone's sake, and I went to see Mr. Mueller once again, this time determined to solve the situation.

"You know," said Mr. Mueller, "it took me a while to accept my daughter as she is. Not because of some prejudice, but because deep down I felt disappointed that I wouldn't have a family. That she'd grow old alone, childless. I know it sounds silly in today's world, but having progeny is such a core part of what makes us human that I believe it was pure instinct." He sighed. "When I came to my senses, I realized that she'd have plenty of options, and when she met you, well, I simply couldn't have been happier."

His words made me feel a tinge of guilt, all of a sudden, as if I were to blame for his daughter's sexuality. "I understand," I said, telling the truth.

"Having you in her life made me feel bright about her future, about our future, and I knew that you could figure things

out, and eventually I'd have
grandchildren, and our house would be
full again—"

"But that is exactly what we're offering
you," I said, trying to meet him half way.

He saw through my bullshit. "You're
not offering me anything. And I'm
accepting nothing."

"Listen," I said. "Don't let her choices
ruin what relationship you have with your
daughter."

"Her choices?"

"Our choices," I said. "Look, you want
family? We can give you family. And you
want acceptance?" I paused, a bit
nervous. "I can give you acceptance."

And I told him about my work in broad
strokes, about the rice, about how half an
hour with our system and he'd be in total
acceptance of our choice, and he'd be
happier, and we'd all be happier.

"You're offering to brainwash me?"

"It's as much brainwashing," I said, "as
any therapy is. As any healing. The
process is just sped up."

"I don't need therapy," he said. "And I
certainly don't need healing." I sensed he
was nearing the end of his patience. Then
he looked me in the eyes. "Perhaps—
perhaps, you could offer the same to her?

Make her see things my way? Our way? Come on, Alice, I know you are reasonable."

I felt sick. Not so much at the suggestion, but rather at this sudden realization, having for a moment imagined Ellie's beliefs changing on the rice, of how crude my offer to Mr. Mueller had been. Who was I to hand a grown man twice my age the solution, neatly wrapped in a brain pill, to his family's supposed ills? I shuddered at my own audacity. If people deserved one thing, it was to be given the time to make their own choices.

I apologized for wasting his time and left. When I got home, I locked myself in the bathroom and sobbed.

Tuning the agents didn't turn out as straightforward as I'd thought. Neutering a century's worth of therapeutical instincts, if heaps of processed datasets can be called that, while still keeping the AIs genuinely helpful was a tight-rope walk.

I stared at anonymized data from the trial. Patient Apple's interaction with our agent after his procedure. Short and to the point. Apple, having had his psychological issues resolved the neurological way, wanted to talk about it no further, especially not with an automated AI therapist. Patient Banana's interaction, much the same. Patient Cranberry's, as if copied and pasted. Done and out in less than five minutes.

Good news was they all seemed healthy and sane.

Bad news was they knew it, and treated our additional help or monitoring the way they'd treat somebody handing them a flyer on the street.

"Durian's psychological profile is as healthy as can be," one agent told me. "There is nothing further I can do. Patient Durian is cured."

I was early one morning in the office, and yet I could hardly focus on what this agent was saying. They all ended up saying the same thing, eventually. All patients succumbed to the rice faster than anything I'd ever seen before, and after a brief sense of vertigo, they quickly accepted their own choice of the neurotechnological option, and moved on with their lives, happier than ever.

I kept track and followed up with as many patients in the trial as possible, to no real use. I wasn't needed, the agents weren't needed.

When I talked to Phillip about this he shook his head.

"Look," he said. "At this point in time we can't afford a repeat of Bolivia."

"I'm aware of the risks."

"We're betting the farm on the rice, Al. We can't afford to mess this up because of sloppy AI-work. We could lose both the agent business and the rice business."

"I said I got it, Phillip."

"We need the agents. We'll need as much feedback as possible, as many people guiding the agents as we can before our worldwide rollout."

"Many people?"

He started at me blankly. Then he furrowed his brow. "Al, the rice works. We're very close to full approval, so we can't botch this now. We're scaling up the operation massively. We're all hands on deck, and at this point, we have thousands of therapists working the software round the clock, all over the world."

In the days before the insemination, in the little time I was home, Ellie and I were like two bored ghosts haunting an apartment where nothing ever happened, passing through each other, barely speaking.

The office didn't feel much more comforting, either. Work itself was progressing well, and the rice was proving better than anyone on the company's board of directors had hoped, but internally a sense of unease was growing.

I dug through our internal files and found some of the many other people looped in as agent-guides. I reached out to a few, under pretext of exchanging notes for the betterment of our work, and found that they were all feeling a similar sense of uncertainty about the product.

"It's too good," one man told me in his office. "I'd never seen people change that way before."

"So why do I feel hesitant?" I asked.

He shrugged. "Because too many people changing too suddenly, too easily, and now you have the whole world changing suddenly, easily. And what does that world look like?"

Phillip was declining my meeting requests, avoiding me in the corridors and offices of our company. Most likely, he'd gotten wind of our conversations and wanted to avoid any potential push-back.

But even I wasn't fully sure what I wanted of him. Perhaps just some reassurance that everything would be alright, that we were not rushing headlong into a mistake, that experienced adults were in charge of steering this ship and that all potential consequences of our product had been fully mapped out.

Clinical trials, lab work, was one thing, but the thought of *scaling up massively* was what gave me and the rest of us a sense of vertigo.

I couldn't help cringing at my last conversation with Mr. Mueller. At the thought of him being a different person, one minute to the next. Of Ellie, being different, one minute to the next. What did my world look like, then?

I sat slumped at the desk in my office. The day was done but I didn't feel like I had anywhere to go, so I just sat there, fiddling with the wire of the charging dock. Nowadays it was all Big This and Big That, and Millions of Data Points and Billions of Datasets and it all went into one blender and out came a perfect agent and a marvel of tool-making with no human required anymore and it was all good for everyone involved. Except what if it wasn't?

What if it wasn't all that great to change people in an instant? What if it wasn't good practice to just do, do, do whatever comes to fucking mind without a second to stop and consider your partner's real feelings? And what if it wasn't such a brilliant fucking idea to turn a future child into a fucking art project?

I stood up, sat back down. I wasn't sure what I was feeling, what I was doing.

I pulled up my computer and scoured for data on the rice trial. It was near the end, but there were a couple of open slots left, and there was one open slot for tomorrow morning at our own lab, and if I shuffled a few meetings around, it would be right on time before our Big Appointment in the afternoon, and I stared at the screen and breathed heavily and my chest hurt and I stood up again and paced the room.

I put on the headset that was charging. "Agent," I said. "Let's go." And on a pristine meadow an agent appeared and I said, "Fuck you, let's go."

"What seems to be the problem? What brings you to me on this fine day?" Slipping right into play-pretend therapy mode, with a tone of voice that I just now realized I hated more than anything in the world.

"Uh huh," I said. "Fuck you."

"Ah, I see it might be anger you're struggling with. Or is this a nervous tic?"

"Fuck you."

"Is there someone in your life that makes you so angry? Are you dealing with a lot of repressed emotions right now? Do you feel the need to shout? To scream?"

"Fuck you," I said. "Fuck you, fuck you."

5.

When I arrived home, Ellie was already sleeping. I watched her silhouette in bed a while, then I softly closed the bedroom door and went down to the kitchen.

I searched the drawers, cabinets, and I sniffed and grimaced at them until I found what I was looking for wrapped in several paper bags. Ellie knew I hated the smell, so she'd wrapped it up nicely. I took the root out and put it in a pot to boil.

I sat on the kitchen table, started scratching at a bit of crust on it from last night's dinner. When the root boiled I poured myself a big mug of the brew. It tasted as horrible as every other time I'd had it in the House of Mueller.

I sipped the drink, thinking of my first date with Ellie. We'd gotten so involved in our conversation we forgot to keep count of the wines. By the end of the night we were so smashed we were walking and swaying and she fell flat on her face right before the entrance to her building and I rushed to pick her up, but she was laughing 'cause it was only a scratch or two on her face, and I joined in and we laughed our heads off right there on the sidewalk. We decided to stay out. I couldn't remember what we talked about. But I knew we'd been awake the whole night, on the curb in front of her building, our sandals in hand, watching the city go to sleep and then slowly shake itself awake, and I remembered nothing except how silly she looked and that sweet, sticky smell of an early summer night.

I finished the drink, then rinsed the mug and shoved the boiled root leftovers to the bottom of the bin. Somehow, I didn't want her knowing had I drunk it.

I thought of Mr. Mueller. Poor Mr. Mueller. Struggling to keep pace with the rest of the world. Just like me. Just like Ellie and just like all of us. As if the World was this separate thing which slipped and squirmed away from our collective hands every time we felt we had a good grasp of it.

I resolved to reach out to him tomorrow after our Big Appointment and make things right between the three of us. Empathy and kindness was what he deserved, and I was sure that given time and acceptance, that empathy and kindness would be reciprocated.

Tomorrow.

But tonight, my head swam, from the tea or the anxiety or both, I did not know.

I went to bed and lay down right next to Ellie.

"I'm just scared, that's all," I whispered, and right then felt the World firmly in my grasp for the first time in a long while. Not letting go, not tonight. I closed my eyes and the whole room was spinning. Tomorrow, I'd decided, I could sleep in, as there would be just one Big Appointment for the day. I held Ellie, hugging her properly for the first time in weeks. And tomorrow, things would spin even harder, and the day after tomorrow even more so, until maybe one day the spinning fully stopped, but for now all the two of us could do was decide to fully plunge into the swirl and start spinning together with the rest of the world, and see where this spinning and squirming but marvelous world took us. "That's all," I said again, and fell asleep.

See Damien Krsteski's story "Core" online at Metaphorosis.
If you liked it, leave a comment. Authors love that!
Remember to subscribe to our e-mail updates so you'll know when new stories are posted.

About the story

I use my stories as excuses to spend time thinking in writing about things I like to think about in general, and my worlds and my characters help me reason better. In "Core", a story revolving around the question of human values and indelible human qualities in an ever-changing world, the fears and anxieties of automation and obsolescence emerge against a backdrop of disorientation with the speed of change. I enjoyed airing out through the characters all of these fears and anxieties and, well, all of my excitement and giddiness, too. I have no doubt I will do so again. The future is exciting, and the world is amazing. And it's not done surprising us.

About the author

Damien Krsteski writes science fiction and develops software. He lives in Berlin.

A word about Suzanne J. Willis

Suzanne J. Willis first appeared in Metaphorosis in January 2017, with "A Nightingale's Map of the City" — still one of my favorite stories we've ever published — a wistful tour de force of beautiful prose and heartfelt emotion. In 2018, she contributed "The Fragments of Others" to our innovative anthology, *Reading 5X5*.

Now, with our final story, she's back with another masterpiece, "This Is My City and I Am Her Song". We've published a lot of great writers over nine years (and you've seen some of my favorites this year), but Suzanne's poetic style may best encapsulate the kind of writing we originally set out to showcase. Enjoy it!

This Is My City and I Am Her Song

Suzanne J. Willis

The clocks stopped still and the night stretched thin as the Siren chased me through my city of shifting secrets. Across canals, and down twisting laneways, until I found myself in the graveyard. It may not have been the most sensible place to hide from a Siren — handmaidens of the Underworld Queen and sisters of Death itself — but it was better than being hunted through the streets like a common thief. I peered out from the mausoleum in which I was huddled, and she appeared in the distance, stalking between the headstones and tombs in the endless night. Cursing silently, I couldn't help but feel the same as I had when I first saw her, fifteen, sixteen years before: overwhelmed by the power radiating from her in subtle waves.

There has never been any rhyme or rhythm to when the Siren visits this city. She has always been peripatetic, unpredictable. I had been a child, no more than four or five, when I first saw her standing at dawn by the canal, under the bridge that connects the marketplace to the Women's Quarter; the quarter, it was said, that was home to shapeshifters and shadows. Her hair was a dark, wild tangle and her black wings arched out from her shoulder blades. I imagined that if she were soaring across sky, they would block out the sun.

My Aunt Zola had raised me on stories, and the one about the Siren I learned by heart. The first time she ever told it to me was on that morning I glimpsed the Siren, under the bridge.

"When she first came here, my little Rosa, I don't know how she made it from the mountains — the shifters of the Women's Quarter would bewitch the on-shore winds to shear away at those sirens who shouldn't be here. But, one morning there she was, huddled under the bridge as though nesting there. All a-tremble and bedraggled as a whelp. Ever since, she comes and goes from the city as she pleases, with no knowing when she might turn up. But whenever she does, strange things happen."

"Stranger than usual?" I would always ask.

"Stranger than the day the sea emptied from the lagoon and left behind the body of the baker's son. Odder than the priestesses who walk the roofs unshod, their feet never touching the earth, and more curious than the cats that guard the ruins of their convent, who howl on the anniversary of the fire that destroyed it." Every time, she had a different answer, telling me the stories of our water-bound city in snippets of the fantastic and horrific. Weaving it to life.

"What kind of things?"

She sighed and touched my cheek. "That first time, a great grey wolf was seen prowling the city, between sunrise and sunset, but there hadn't been wolves in these parts for over one hundred years. Other animals who were left outside after dark — seabirds and cats, mostly — were found petrified, their feathers or fur crusted with salt. They lined the canals like statues. And there were *other* things, too much for young ears to hear."

"And the lady with the black wings?"

"The last place she always went was across the bridge to the Women's Quarter. After that, the animals stopped turning to statues, and the wolves no longer howled at midnight. None of that has happened in your lifetime, I know, but that doesn't mean that she stays away, as you've seen. And she doesn't find herself here by accident, Rosa. No, she is looking for something."

The mournful call of a nightbird calling out across the tombs broke my reverie. It was the only sound in the graveyard; the quiet calm of night made me nervous. *I know what she is looking for, and she hasn't found it yet,* I whispered to Zola's memory, closing my hand over the precious cargo in my pocket. I imagined her telling me to walk away, to forget. Cowering there, not knowing when the Siren might find me, I was sorely tempted to do just that.

Then she walked from the shadows under the weeping trees, making her way between the gravestones. Watching her, not only did I feel the same, but the Siren looked the same as she had that first day

I saw her, so long ago, down by the canal. Haunted, and tired, too. It made me wonder how long she had been looking for that very-precious thing (for she had surely been looking long before she reached our city) and what would happen when she found me with it. If only Aunt Zola were still here, I could tell her I knew exactly what it was that the Siren was after, and ask Zola's help, ask her *what next*. For while I held the lost Siren's secret in my cloak pocket, I had not a clue as to what to do with it.

"Never rely on any man to support you," Aunt Zola had always said, for as long as I could remember. "We will find you a good trade, my girl, and there will be no marriage to yoke you." She was my maternal aunt, the one who took me in when it became clear that my parents would never return from their expedition beyond the mountains. I knew Zola blamed my father for the disappearance of her sister, and that she wouldn't risk the same for me. That suited me just fine. Marriage and children never much interested me, having to answer to a man even less than that. I had harboured a secret hope that Zola might pack us up and move into the Women's Quarter, even hinted at it once or twice. *That's not somewhere just anyone can live,* Zola had whispered, shivering at the thought. *Witches and medicine women and shapeshifters belong to those streets. It is not for the likes of us.* She didn't mention the rumours about what else might live there. For some said it was a refuge for those female monsters who walked the boundary between worlds, between human and beast, between story and reality. She didn't mention it, and I knew better than to ask again.

So, at seventeen, she sent me to the artist Leonardo as his apprentice. The only man, I would add, who not only did not mind an errant girl as his student, but seemed to prefer it. He treated me like an equal as I sharpened my mind with the books he gave me to read; as I coarsened my hands building machines of his invention. It was my third year with him when he first left me alone over the winter. Zola had been dead some two years by then, leaving me without any family to anchor me in the world, though Leonardo was kind and welcoming. I had the feeling he would have given me more responsibility sooner, but that he waited until Zola's death was not so raw and my grief had healed over a bit.

My first task on his departure was to tidy and secure everything, order it for his return in the spring. His notebooks were easy enough, re-filed into chronological order. Then there were the small instruments he worked on in his office, the ones that the science school commissioned to use in their experiments. Those went in glass-fronted cases, locked away from the cold salty air, which would rust their gears and jam their delicate mechanisms. Last was the workshop. The smell of sawdust was warm, comforting, as I put the tools back into place and covered the machines he was working on with large dust sheets. Before my apprenticeship, I had never realised that machines could be beautiful. But the ones made by Leonardo — all wood and canvas, gears and hinges — were like works of art, their shapes inspired by nature, their purpose sometimes unclear but certain to move the city ever-forward.

As I covered the last of them, I noticed that the door to the annex workshop, where Leonardo worked alone, was ajar. I walked over, reached out to close the door, then drew my hand back. "Hello?" I called softly, for it did not seem as though the workshop was empty. There was no answer, but, from the darkness, it felt as though someone had invited me in. I picked up one of the gas lamps and walked through the door, then clicked the taper mechanism my master had created to light the large lamp hanging from the ceiling.

My breath caught in my throat. The machine in that little room was like nothing else I had ever seen. Laid across three saw-horses was a horizontal frame, bookended by handholds at one end and a swallow's tail at the other, large enough for a full-grown adult to lie in. A tan leather harness joined the base to the upper struts, upon which was fixed an enormous pair of wings. Unlike the other machines in the workshop, they were not made of canvas, but of glossy black feathers, each one oiled and preened and perfect. From the wing-joints ran fine copper wires, downward into a nest woven of scraps of twigs and hair and the soft reeds that grew at the canal edges. Had Leonardo (for this he had made, surely, for himself) been strapped into the contraption, that nest would have sat against the centre of his chest. And in that nest lay an egg.

The likes of which should not, *could not*, have existed.

Yet there it was. As big as an ostrich egg, it was dark, grey-green and lit gently from within. The light itself pulsed, and it seemed as though there was an electrical storm trapped inside it, dark clouds passing over its surface. The shell was veined in gold, hair-fine and intricate. I hovered my hand above it and it felt warm; blood-heat. The *life* within it was irresistible and I began to close my fingers around it —

"Is it not exquisite?" Leonardo's voice was soft, unaccusatory.

I turned around, my cheeks warm with shame. But he simply smiled at me as he walked over and gently picked up the egg. I gasped, for as he picked it up, all the feathers from those magnificent wings disappeared, leaving behind wings made of wood frame and canvas. I must have looked like a half-wit, standing there gaping at the flying machine that, while still remarkable, looked no different than Leonardo's other workshop creations.

He stowed the treasure in his coat. "I'm sorry, Rosa, I should never have been so careless and left this where you might find it. I must ask you to forget that you ever saw this egg. Owning it..." he shook his head, paused as though looking for the right words, "Actually, understanding it, seeking its help, takes much knowledge and discipline, and a command of magics that few possess. Without that, it is a dangerous object to be in the presence of, much less attempt to use. And there is not a soul in this city who would not try to use it, given the chance. You felt its pull, no?"

I nodded and smiled at my master as he left the workshop, trying to disguise the fact that, no matter what he said, the egg had already worked its magic on me. That night, I dreamed I was flying, coal black wings extending out from my shoulder blades, far into the sky. Below me, our city spread out, its secrets laid open to me in all their complexity and wonder. From the streets and the waterways came a lament, sad and terrible, composed of notes not of this world. Then a cry rang out and the dream went dark.

A pounding on the door awoke me from my sleep the next morning, just as the sky was lightening. The young messenger at the door as I opened it looked grave, almost fearful.

"There has been an accident, Ms Rosa. Your master, Leonardo…" He trailed off and I did not want to ask what had happened. His tone, the early hour, already told me that it was not good.

"He has no family, miss," said the boy, each word accompanied by a puff of mist from his mouth in the freezing dawn, "so, you see, they need you to formally identify the body and assist with —"

I held up my hand, not wanting to hear anything else at that moment. My knees felt weak and I was light-headed, as though the world had shifted but I was still on its old kilter. He reached out to steady me, but I drew myself up and waved his hands away. My parents, Aunt Zola, now Leonardo. I had had enough of the clumsy kindnesses that come with death to last me a lifetime. The losses piled on one another like autumn leaves.

If the boy did not touch me, I could just about keep my emotions inside.

Wrapped in my warmest coat, I followed the messenger boy out into the morning, trying not to slip on the damp cobbles or lose him in the fog as he hurried through the streets. Already, the sounds of the floating markets and the boatmen rang through the air, waking the city and setting it about its day. It smelled of woodsmoke and low tide and just a little bit of the snow that already capped the distant mountains. A shiver passed through me that had nothing to do with the early winter. Though I had lost someone else, someone I had grown to love, the world went on.

At last, we arrived at a little bridge in a hidden laneway that looked rarely, if ever, used. Lawmen and women milled about, some taking notes, others measuring the scene for who-knows-what purpose. The boy spoke with one of the lawmen and, as I looked about, I realised what the boy must have been saying when I had cut him off so abruptly in the doorway. They needed my assistance to *retrieve Leonardo's body*. For the bridge did not just lead to just any part of the city. It led to the Women's Quarter.

That particular quarter was not somewhere that just anyone could, or should, wander. Witches and practitioners of other feminine arts did not frighten me so much as the *others* who had disappeared from the world and made their home in this mysterious part of the city. The shapeshifters and mermaids. The descendants of Delphyne, who kept their snake tails hidden but still breathed fire at the first sign of trouble. Harpies and their hidden staircase straight to the underworld. All, it seemed, except sirens, who still guarded the mountaintops and desert plains.

I thought of *her*. I thought of his flying machine and its midnight wings. I wondered.

And I wondered what on earth Leonardo could have been doing here, and why it had brought him his death.

The next few minutes passed in a blur. There was a conversation with the lawmen, some brief and useless directions, and absolutely no hint of what I might encounter. Armed with next to nothing, I crossed the bridge as the little crowd fell silent, so the only sound was my boots clomping on the cobbles and the current lazily lapping beneath it. The little square on the other side seemed no different from any of the hundreds in the city proper. Except that as I gazed down the laneways, I saw shop signs that were unfamiliar, doorways shimmering into sight then back into the shadows. Down one of those laneways walked a group of seven women, all in long, dark cloaks. Six carried a stretcher bearing a body and the seventh followed close behind them. A cry hitched in my throat. I swallowed it down again, and it felt as though, in the odd stillness, I was laid bare for all to see.

The seventh woman beckoned to me from the laneway as the six stretcher-bearers walked into the square and waited. When I reached her, we were out of sight of the lawmen and women. I had never felt so utterly alone and exposed. The woman peered at me from under her hood. Her face seemed to shift between human and vulpine, not quite settling on either. She looked sad, her eyes red as though she had been crying.

"Did you know Leonardo?" I whispered.

"I am Villanelle. Your master was a friend to us here. He spoke highly of you, Rosa. Don't look so surprised," she smiled, "he had hopes for you. But we've not much time. Take this — it is not safe here." The fox-woman Villanelle reached under her cloak, withdrew a bundle and placed it in my hands. I did not need to ask what it was, for I could feel it, pulsing in my hands, a storm barely contained by a golden-veined shell.

"What happened to him?"

Villanelle shook her head. "He held that egg for longer than should have been possible. It has a different effect on everyone anyone who comes into contact with it. He came to broker a deal —" she broke off and looked around, though I could hear nothing but the distant flap of wings and call of morning birds.

"The Siren agreed, many centuries ago, to protect our city, for here we gave refuge to creatures, monsters, that were hunted elsewhere. In return for that protection, we had to hide something very valuable inside this. It took a strong person to take custody of it..."

"Leonardo," I said.

"As his apprentice, and he with no family, the natural laws say that this must pass to you." She brushed my cheek, and made a sigil in the air between us, muttering words in a language I did not understand. Panic fluttered in me, but something told me that this was not a curse, but protection. "Tell no-one about it. You must hold onto it and keep it from she who seeks it."

"The siren?" The words were out of my mouth before I had even formed the thought. But I *knew* this was what she sought, what all Zola's stories talked about, just as surely as I knew my own name.

Her eyebrows rose in surprise, then she smiled. "Leonardo was right about you. Yes, she is here in the city, so you must avoid her at all costs. Do not let her find you. Or it."

So I run from her this time. Then what? Am I to keep this forever? I wanted to ask more, but she ushered me out of the laneway and into the square. Villanelle pulled back the shroud and I looked at his face, then nodded. It was only as I led the stretcher-bearers back across the bridge that I began to cry.

How on earth was I to try to avoid a Siren? One, no less, who was wandering the world in search of the very thing that I now possessed. I sat in the workshop, before Leonardo's flying machine, turning the egg over in my hands. Many of the women of this city were known to walk into the Women's Quarter as death approached them — but Villanelle had said Leonardo was there to *broker a deal*. Had someone murdered him for the treasure that I now held?

Well, I wouldn't find any answer simply sitting and wondering. Taking a deep breath, I walked over to the flying machine and placed the egg gently in the nest, waiting for the wings to transform into the black, feathered masterpieces I had seen not twenty-four hours earlier. And waited. And waited. But the wings stayed canvas and wood, and the machine did not feel as *alive* as it had the day before.

Pulling the egg from the nest, I took it back to my rooms above the workshop and sat by the window, holding it in my lap. Through the open window floated the sounds of the city; the market vendors and the boatmen; the street musicians with mournful violin and haunting flutes; the everyday chatter of people for whom life had not just changed overnight. The Villanelle had said that the fragile egg affected everyone differently. Perhaps that gift of flight was only for Leonardo. I closed my eyes, turning the egg over and over in my hands.

Against my palms, the Siren's treasure pulsed, steady and strong. Images floated in and out of my mind, as though I was sifting through dreams. A black sand beach stretched under glorious grey skies, upon which sat seven Sirens, singing down passing ships while their cousins, the mermaids, flitted through the waves before the ships crashed to the shore. Under the rain-heavy clouds, the souls of the men flew, shaped as crow and albatross and fledging gull. The song of the sirens did not just mean death; it was transformative, transmutative. Then, a city made of white and black stone, rising from an island, a shack, the humble beginnings of a village; rising and spreading, until the death song of the Sirens rang through the streets, followed by a rain of fire from the sky. Parliaments of animals and birds gathered to create, break, remake the world. Time stretching and contracting, life and death dancing. And, at the centre of it all, the storm-egg beating like a heart. The dreams danced over me like rain.

The howl of a wolf made me open my eyes suddenly. The light outside was fading and the western sky was soft and gold as a cool wind blew in through the window. In the little moment between day and evening, the musicians stopped, the market was packed up, the people closed their shutters and doors. And a song threaded its way through the streets, over the canals, on the back of the wolf's howl and the twilight. It was the lost Siren calling to the egg. Emotion rose in my throat and I began to cry again. There was a delicate despondency to the refrain; loss was woven through it. She had been looking for that egg for a very long time. When she sang — don't believe, for a second, that Sirens only sing for death — the egg moved restlessly in my hand, as though the storms inside it were gathering and waiting to burst. I dared not think about what might happen if they did. All the same, the fox-woman Villanelle had been adamant that the egg should remain in the city. But that did not mean with me. Perhaps I could hide it...

I knew enough to know that borderland creatures are tricksy things, so I could not trust the ordinary to tell me how to find a hiding place, how to outrun her. Back down in the workshop, I took out the large map of the city that Leonardo had completed just last spring, and traced my finger over the canals and laneways, the little islands and larger districts. Everyone in the city had a small story about *her*, heard from their parents or grandparents, or learnt through their own encounter. In a city of secrets and wonder, it was the Siren who was the most mysterious of all, perhaps because she was not ours. I tried to draw all the stories I had heard together, weaving them into a long thread that would lead me through the labyrinth. I traced the city with my fingertip, whispering as the darkness gathered outside.

Once upon a time, the sirens and mermaids were as one, until the sirens took to the skies and the mermaids to the deepest seas. That is why she is always seen by the water...

My mother was first violinist in the orchestra, and she heard an other-worldly singing under her window when she was practising one night; when she looked out, there she was, sitting in the peach tree and trilling like a little bird...

Like all half-human monsters, Sirens are borderland creatures, said to violate the boundaries between life and death, this world and the Underworld, the rules of belonging and place...

I went on like that for an hour or so, making notes, narrowing down where I thought the Siren might be and where she could not reach. I had the egg sat on the table beside me, unwilling to let it out of my sight. Somewhat absentmindedly, I reached out and rested my hand on it, its shell still warm to the touch. Without quite knowing why, a sob rose in my throat. How short life suddenly seemed, how insignificant... all those I had loved — my parents when I was just a child, my aunt who raised me, Leonardo who had given me knowledge and craft and my second home — were gone. What of their lives unfinished? Turning to grab a handkerchief for my tears, the sad emptiness that had weighted me so suddenly disappeared just as quickly. As soon as I took my hand off the egg.

"What could I do with more time?" I whispered to it. Beneath the shell, the storm raged and lightning struck. *Anything*, the storm promised. The map swam in and out of focus, changing and morphing, some islands sinking beneath the waters and others springing up in their wake. It was as though I were looking at five hundred years running through it in a few seconds; perhaps I was. Then it settled back into its current, familiar state. The shadow of a tiny, winged figure walking along the banks of the little canal on which Leonardo's workshop passed over the parchment, moth-delicate, then was gone.

I grabbed the egg, threw on my cloak and ran out into the night.

Only, the night was different in ways that I could not imagine. Although I have lived in this city my whole life, I managed to find bridges that I did not know existed, pass through neighbourhoods dark and mysterious, as though they had become stuck in another era and only emerged when needs must. Without a doubt, she was close on my heels as I wound my way through the city. Each time the swoop of her wings, or the brisk clack of talons on the cobblestones told me she nearly had me, a turn right or left would take me down an odd path and into safety, however temporary. I imagined Leonardo creating his beautiful map in this same way, though I'm sure that the minutes did not stop, the night did not *pause* in the same way.

It was as though the world were underwater and I was viewing it, interacting with it, through a thin pane of glass. As though I had shifted into a narrow passageway in between the world and the natural forces that kept it going. In a crowded laneway, people moved unusually slow around me, their voices sounding far away. After what seemed like two or three hours of walking and hiding in shadows, I passed our astrological clock and it read 11.37 — the same time that I had left my rooms.

I turned away from the clock, through a passageway and out into a square that sparkled with soft candlelight from hurricane lamps hanging over tables set with wine and fruits, spiced meats and fragrant soups. The air was curiously still, redolent with the scents of the wedding feast. Musicians played a tune I could not hear; some guests were dancing, others seated, smiling and chatting. Looking at the wedding feast was like watching insects being encased in sap that would slowly turn to amber. A cool wind blew through the square, blowing the candles.

Music seemed to explode in the night, and I was part of the world again.

The dancing made my head spin. Across the square, there was a flash of a red tail, a dog or a fox perhaps, drawn out by the smell of the food.

"You have the egg." I froze at the sound of the Siren's low voice. Her breath was soft on the back of my neck.

I turned slowly, my heart in my throat. She seemed to fill the sky even though she was the same height as me. Those black wings arced upwards from her shoulder blades, and she stretched them outward, a bird readying for flight. I felt a pang for Leonardo and the creation he would never get to test.

"Why do you want it?"

Her eyes flashed and my knees turned to water. "You might be Leonardo's apprentice, child, but you have not earned the right to ask that." She moved towards me and I tensed, ready for her to strike.

"You knew Leonardo?"

She smiled at me and it was surprisingly gentle. Before she could answer, the fox I had seen earlier streaked towards us from the shadows. With her last few steps, she grew, shifted and came to a stop as Villanelle, standing between me and the Siren.

"You would take back the egg and see our city ruined?" I was surprised at the sadness in Villanelle's words.

"You put too much stock in the old stories, sister. They have become twisted, over the centuries, and make you and your kind so unsure of your own place in the world. This city is more yours than it ever was mine..."

The Siren continued in her lilting voice, lulling Villanelle as though mesmerising her. I took my chance — while she was so focussed on the fox-woman, I slipped into the shadows, taking the egg with me. When I could no longer hear her, time slowed and I stepped into the in-between spaces once again. I knew, then, where I was headed. To the city's cemetery, a water-bound island of earthly graves and fiery cremation furnaces. Earth, fire, water — where better to hide a secret from a creature of the air? I pushed away the niggling worry that had uncurled when the Siren spoke to Villanelle — the worry that, perhaps, I should not be hiding what was rightfully hers at all.

The iron gate was set in an ancient stone wall, and curlicued with vines and autumn leaves. I tied the boat I had borrowed to the tiny pier, my arms aching from the unfamiliar motion of rowing. I wondered if Villanelle had been entirely enchanted — or worse — by the Siren. I hoped she was safe.

Beyond the gate, my footfalls were silent on the soft grass, the cemetery's angels and weeping women and ancient mausoleums limned in moonlight. I looked for somewhere safe, secure. A mausoleum, I had decided, would be the perfect hiding place. I walked until I found one whose gate had long since rusted and the names of its dead had been weathered away. As I ducked inside, I heard the rustle of wings, the footfalls of clawed feet.

How?

But, of course, I already knew that. The egg was calling to her and I might be able to outrun her for a while, but never truly lose her. Perhaps she was a bit like me — alone in the world. At least I had my city as an anchor, the home I had known all my life, with reminders of Zola and Leonardo and the parents I knew only through stories echoing through it. Perhaps she was chasing after *her* anchor, and it was calling out, to be heard. Found. I shifted uncomfortably; a discomfort that had nothing to do with the cold stone or the cramped tomb.

What if Villanelle was right, and giving the Siren what she needed would take away the last part of belonging that I had? Then again, all those years that the Siren had searched the city, looking for what I was now complicit in keeping from her — to keep it would be to add to her suffering. I don't think anyone could have held onto the egg for the time that I had and not understand that.

I had plenty of questions, but not a single answer. So, I simply sat, as still as I could, and looked up into the night sky for a long, long time. Expecting her to appear at any moment and rip the egg from my grasp. But there were no sounds of her growing any closer; no keening for her egg, which sat in my hand, beating softly. And time continued to stretch and move so imperceptibly as to have almost stopped. Above me the moon, hanging like a scythe, did not continue her journey and the stars stopped their endless circle. It seemed that the egg was making good on the promise it had made to me earlier, when I was silly enough to allow it to know my own sadness. With that one simple question — *What could I do with more time?* — I had revealed myself to it. And with its answer, it had caught me like a fish in a net.

Anything.

There I was, crouched like a cur, in the cemetery where more time was as useful as a flying machine to a fish. I could spend forever there, wondering about what to do, about what was right or wrong, *or* I could jump, and find out.

I stepped out of the cold tomb. The Siren was nowhere to be seen, though I could feel her, traversing this hinterland between the living and the dead. I shivered. The truth of it was, standing so close to death terrified me; all that nothingness, stretching out forever.

"Hello?" My voice quivered. The egg skipped a beat, an arrhythmic tell that *she* must be close by. "I'm sorry I ran from you —"

Behind me, the rustle of folding wings and the soft crunch of talons in the gravelly path. I turned, and there she was, all wild hair and starbright eyes.

"Did you know of Leonardo's flying machine?" I blurted out.

Her smile was unexpectedly beautiful. "Oh, yes. We had plans, your master and I, to traverse the skies together. Oh! You are surprised?" She touched my face gently, her fingertips cool against my skin. Realisation washed over her face. "You did not know about us... He went to Villanelle to negotiate its return, you know." She gestured to my pocket, with its exquisitely frangible cargo.

"Was he..." I couldn't finish my question. Murder is such an ugly word.

"No one would ever have harmed him. He met a most ordinary end. The streets were icy and he slipped, hitting his head on the stones. He did not suffer."

"Why did he not just give you the egg?"

"Can you not think of any reason?"

I wracked my brains, ran the old stories through my mind. Oh! "He did not really want to let it go! And you can't just take it back, because it must be freely given." I thanked Aunt Zola silently for her fireside stories.

The Siren smiled. "He spoke of you, Rosa. Never did he dream, he told me, that he would find a student who he could imagine one day taking over from him. And then he found you."

Had she decided to pluck one of her feathers and poke me with it, she could easily have knocked me over. "I have no special talent! If I study his notebooks, his teachings, for my whole life, I could not come close to —"

"You underestimate yourself. Did you not take the egg into your care, and elude me for a whole night? Has it not listened to you and stretched out time according to your wishes?"

It hadn't occurred to me that that meant I was something special, and I was not convinced simply because she said so. "I was just doing as I was told."

"Were you, now? And what do you think our Leonardo would value more — an apprentice who would simply do what she was told, or an independent thinker?"

"I will assume that question is rhetorical." We smiled at one another, then, sharing the memory of him for just a moment.

"Villanelle, all the women who work their magic and keep this city safe, they believe that their magic depends on the egg. That if it was returned to me, their magic would wither and die."

I put my hand over the egg, warm and safe under my cloak, even though I didn't need to do that to know its power. "Why would they think that?" I whispered.

She stretched her wings, looking up at the unmoving stars as she did so, then folding them against her back again. Under that sliver of moon, she looked like a goddess who was tired of the world she had created. "Because inside the egg lies my death."

I was jealous that she was able to evade death in that way — and covetous of it, too.

"And now you want to die?" I was incredulous that anybody would go *looking* for death. Around us, the dead were silent in their graves, but I was sure that, if they heard us, they would be thinking the very same thing.

"Death is not the ending that you seem to think it is."

"I think our friends here would disagree." I motioned towards the graves stretching out on all sides of us. "I want to do the right thing, but I don't know what that is." I hated how small my voice sounded, how small I felt.

"I can't decide that for you, no matter how much I would like to. Just know, Rosa, that I am very, very tired."

She looked older than anyone I had ever met. And the way she was looking at me, somewhere between imploring and pitying, seemed to shift my thinking, and I realised... It did not matter how much time I had — whether it was another hour, or ten years, or two hundred years — it could not undo hurt, or take away pain. It could not make up for the time already lost. It could not change the fact that Leonardo walked that particular path that night, or that my parents left their only child to bring the monster-hunters to justice. All those things were immutable and done, never to be redone. And no matter how much time there was, it would never be enough, for there would always be things unfinished. There would always be an end. For the Siren, for the city, for me.

I held out the egg to her. "Who am I — who are we — to keep this from you?"

Who was I to stop time or say a city should not sink beneath the waves?

As she reached out for it, the town square clocks chimed thirteen and a cold breeze that smelled of winter swept through the cemetery. The tempest inside the eggshell roared and raged, cracking it open and sweeping us both up in its arms. I felt like I was falling forever as the Siren's feathers drifted from her wings, spinning around us as black snow. Unspooling time. Closing my eyes against the raging winds, in my mind's eye I saw an aerie atop an ancient mountain, spearing toward the sky. In that nest, Siren chicks muddled and tumbled and made room for the new egg that formed there at their feet.

Death is not the ending that you seem to think it is.

Her voice, a voice that bewitched sailors to their deaths and sung a city safe, echoed in my ears as darkness dragged me down.

When I awoke, the sky in the east was pale and the sounds of the city waking joined the first birdsong. Not only was my home still standing, it felt as though it were stretching outwards, expanding the laneways and digging roots through the sandy bed of the lagoon in search of new ways, new worlds, like a radicle searching for the sun. Somewhere in the labyrinth of canals and secrets, the fox-women of the Women's Quarter were weaving new stories. Of the Siren who finally found her death inside an eggshell; of how Villanelle and her kind learned that it set them free from old superstitions; of letting the future unfold anew, untethered from the past. As for me, I sat in the early morning winter sun and wove the hours, days, and years the egg had given me through my thoughts, my memories, my dreams, the way a mermaid braids starfish in her hair.

I would keep its gift of time with me as my companion, let it teach me to bite like stars on the edge of night, and to gamble like devils with their last soul to lose. And when my ending comes, I will turn what is left of it back out into the world, scattered like seaglass on the shore for another lonely, lost girl to find and learn what it is to live.

See Suzanne J. Willis's story "This Is My City and I Am Her Song" online at Metaphorosis. If you liked it, leave a comment. Authors love that! Remember to subscribe to our e-mail updates so you'll know when new stories are posted.

About the story

I came across a black and white photograph online of a woman standing by what looked like a little bridge in Venice. She had wild hair and black wings arching out from her back, with a melancholy look on her face. It looked to me as though she had lost something precious and was searching for it, high and low. That was the genesis of my Siren, and this began as a flash fiction piece. As sometimes happens, the story needed much more space than a thousand or so words, so I kept writing, until I found out what it was she was looking for (even I didn't know when I started the story!).

I was already a few thousand words into another story about desert-dwelling sirens, so had read a lot about their mythology — their connection to the underworld and death, an alluring nature, a seemingly-deadly beauty — and what struck me was that despite their destructive nature, they are have protective qualities. So, that was something that I wanted to explore.

Sirens are fierce, independent, reliant on no-one; these are things that my protagonist, Rosa, had to learn at a very early age. This has the capacity to harden her, but instead it leaves her curious, trying to understand the world from a different angle. In writing this story I wondered how Rosa would be affected by the mystery of the Siren. And what might happen when they finally met.

A question for the author

Q: What's your writing schedule?

A: My writing fits into the spaces around work, family, and friends! So, I tend to write in snippets — an evening here, a lunchtime there. It is somewhat haphazard, but it seems to work. However, I do have one Monday per fortnight off work and this is my dedicated writing time — that Monday is sacred and nothing else is ever scheduled on that day. I find that the best way for me to find my way into a story is to always begin with notes written in my journals or notebooks (beautiful notebooks are my weakness!), then shape the story from there. Of course, the first draft is the slowest part, but my editing schedule is much quicker — every night until the story feels right to go out into the world.

About the author

Suzanne is a lawyer and writer who lives in Melbourne, Australia. Her spare moments are spent with words and music, her stories inspired by fairytales, ghost stories, and all things strange. Suzanne's first short story collection, *Of Starfish Tides and Other Tales* was released in 2022 by Trepidatio Publishing.

A word about Carol Wellart

I'm not an artist, at least visually. I can imagine all sorts of fantastic scenes, but as for getting them down on paper or screen? A child's stick figures would look good compared to my efforts.

That was a stumbling block for the magazine initially. I can't draw, and didn't know any artists. Happily, we were able to attract a wide range of talented folk starting midway through the first year, and the problem was largely solved.

What we didn't have, though, was any kind of signature, standard look, and occasionally a scheduled artist would fall through for one reason or another. We found the solution in Carol Wellart.

Carol did her first cover for us early on, in 2017, and quickly became one of our regularly returning artists, with seven covers between 2017 and 2021. It would have been more if I hadn't felt obligated to work in people who'd been waiting patiently in our artists' roster.

For 2022, though, I asked Carol to provide *all* the covers for the year, and happily she agreed. For 2023, she provided half of all covers — again because I felt an obligation to give a chance to other artists on the roster.

The four cover artists for 2024 are among my favorites of the artists we've worked with. But if there's one artist who could be said to be Metaphorosis' principal artist, it's Carol Wellart, who in addition to the magazine provided the cover art for our anthology *Score*. This final cover for Metaphorosis is a beauty again, based on E.C. Dorgan's story, "The New Western".

Thanks, Carol. We owe you!

Be sure to check out Carol's other beautiful work at **carolwellart.com**.

Farewell

All things end. This is the last issue of *Metaphorosis*. After nine years, one hundred issues, 2.3 million words, 400-some stories, 326 authors, and 28 artists, the magazine is closing its doors.

It's been a lot of fun working with all those authors and artists and seeing their finished work go out to meet the world. I'm proud of the quality of the magazine we produced and of the fact that for some of these authors, *Metaphorosis* was their first publication or paying venue. I've been thrilled to see 'our' creators go on to bigger and better things.

While the magazine is closing, the press isn't; we have plans for more anthologies and projects in the coming years. Keep your eyes out for them.

In the meantime, our back issues are all available and all the stories and podcasts are online. And if you miss fresh, new SFF stories, consider supporting some of the other great magazines that are out there.

Morris Allen
Editor

Copyright

Title information

Metaphorosis Oct-Dec 2024

ISSN: 2573-136X (online)
ISBN: 978-1-64076-284-8 (e-book)
ISBN: 978-1-64076-285-5 (paperback)

Publisher

Metaphorosis
a magazine of speculative fiction

Metaphorosis Magazine is an imprint of
Metaphorosis Publishing
Neskowin, OR, USA

www.metaphorosis.com

"Metaphorosis" is a registered trademark.

Discounts available

Substantial discounts are available for educational institutions, including writing workshops. Discounts are also available for quantity purchases. For details, contact Metaphorosis at metaphorosis.com/about

Metaphorosis Publishing

Metaphorosis offers beautifully written science fiction and fantasy. Our imprints include:

Metaphorosis Magazine
Plant Based Press
Verdage
Vestige
Joyful Heave

You can also find us:
@metaphorosis.bsky.social (Bluesky)
@Metaphorosis@writing.exchange (Mastodon)
www.facebook.com/metaphorosis

See more about some of our books on the following pages.

Metaphorosis Magazine

Metaphorosis

a magazine of speculative fiction

Metaphorosis is an online speculative fiction magazine dedicated to quality writing. We publish an original story every week, along with author bios, interviews, and notes on story origins.

We also publish monthly print and e-book issues, as well as yearly Best of and Complete anthologies.

Come and see us online at magazine.Metaphorosis.com.

Plant Based Press

plant
based
press

Vegan-friendly science fiction and fantasy, including anthologies of the year's best SFF stories, from 2016-2020.

Chambers of the Heart
speculative stories
by
B. Morris Allen

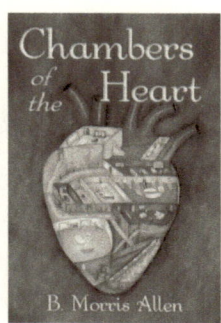

A heart that's a building, a dog that's a program, a woman sinking irretrievably — stories about love, loss, and motion.

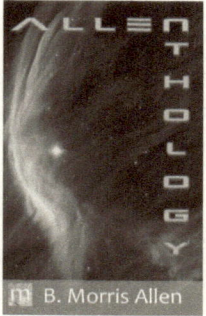

Susurrus

A darkly romantic story of magic, love, and suffering.

Allenthology: Volume I

Including three full collections of SFF stories.

Verdage

Science fiction and fantasy books for writers — full of great stories, often with an additional focus on the craft of speculative fiction writing.

Reading 5X5 x3

Changes

How do stories move from 'maybe' to published?

Here are 15 case studies of stories published in *Metaphorosis* magazine.

Reading 5X5 x2

Duets

How do authors' voices change when they collaborate?

A round-robin of five talented science fiction and fantasy authors collaborating with each other and writing solo.

Including stories by Evan Marcroft, David Gallay, J. Tynan Burke, L'Erin Ogle, and Douglas Anstruther.

Score

an SFF symphony

An anthology with an emotional score from the heights of joy to the depths of despair – but always with a little hope shining through.

Reading 5X5

Five stories, five times

See how different writers take on the same material.

Reading 5X5

Writers' Edition

Two extra stories, the story seed, and authors' notes on writing.

Vestige

Novelettes, novellas, and novels by Metaphorosis authors.

The Nocturnals
Mariah Montoya

Night is Dangerous.
Day is deadly.

Where day and night last thirty years, humans move constantly stay ahead of the night and cruel Nocturnals that call it home. But a boy is lost out there.